Readers love the Carlisle Fire series by ANDREW GREY

Through the Flames

"I really liked this ending much better and it gave you those warm, fuzzy feelings of hope."

—Love Bytes

"If you like sexy firemen, hot contractors, enemies to lovers, forced proximity, cute dogs, and a touch of suspense, you will love this."

—TTC Books and More

Up in Flames

"I love being able to say 'I know that place' as the characters take us around the town."

—Sparkling Book Reviews

By Andrew Grey

Accompanied by a Waltz
All for You
Between Loathing and Love
Borrowed Heart
Buck Me
Buried Passions
Catch of a Lifetime
Chasing the Dream
Crossing Divides
Dedicated to You
Dominant Chord
Don't Let Go
Dutch Treat
Eastern Cowboy
Half a Cowboy
Hard Road Back
Hunks of the Month
In Search of a Story
Lost and Found
Love at First Swipe
New Tricks
Noble Intentions
North to the Future
One Good Deed
On Shaky Ground
Only the Brightest Stars
Past His Defenses
Path Not Taken
The Playmaker
Pulling Strings
Rebound
Reunited
Running to You

Saving Faithless Creek
Second Go-Round
Shared Revelations
Steal My Heart
Survive and Conquer
Three Fates
To Have, Hold, and Let Go
Turning the Page
Twice Baked
Unfamiliar Waters
Whipped Cream

ART
Legal Artistry • Artistic Appeal
Artistic Pursuits • Legal Tender

BAD TO BE GOOD
Bad to Be Good • Bad to Be Worthy
Bad to Be Noble • Bad to Be Merry

BOTTLED UP
The Best Revenge • Bottled Up
Uncorked • An Unexpected Vintage

BRONCO'S BOYS
Inside Out • Upside Down
Backward • Round and Round
Over and Back • Above and Beyond

THE BULLRIDERS
A Wild Ride • A Daring Ride
A Courageous Ride

Published by DREAMSPINNER PRESS
www.dreamspinnerpress.com

FROM *the* FLAMES
ANDREW GREY

Published by
DREAMSPINNER PRESS

8219 Woodville Hwy #1245
Woodville, FL 32362 USA
www.dreamspinnerpress.com

This is a work of fiction. Names, characters, places, and incidents either are the product of author imagination or are used fictitiously, and any resemblance to actual persons, living or dead, business establishments, events, or locales is entirely coincidental.

From the Flames
© 2025 Andrew Grey

Cover Art
© 2025 L.C. Chase
http://www.lcchase.com
Cover content is for illustrative purposes only and any person depicted on the cover is a model.

Trade Paperback ISBN: 9781641088725
Digital ISBN: 9781641088718
Trade Paperback published November 2025
v. 1.0

Chapter 1

THE APARTMENT was finally quiet now that April and Grant were asleep in bed. Willy Daugherty sat on the sofa in the living room with the television on low, because he had learned the hard way how sound traveled through this place. Shortly after moving in a year ago, he had been watching a movie when an explosion onscreen brought Grant running out of his room and leaping onto his lap, and cries from April, who was then fourteen months old. Now, once the kids were in bed, the volume never went above ten, but still he cringed at the loud parts.

The last thing four-year-old Grant ever wanted was to go to bed. He was active from the time he got up in the morning until Willy managed to coax him into bed with at least two stories and a song. But it used to take longer, so at least things were improving. April was a sweetheart, spending her days trying to keep up with her older brother, so usually she fell right asleep.

Willy smiled as he thought of the kids—his kids—and then turned his attention to the television. He'd found a movie on Netflix, but it was probably a bad idea at this time of night because of what he knew was coming: screaming and dragon cries as Millie Bobbie Brown was about to be sacrificed to the dragon. He turned off the television and carefully padded down the short hallway to his room, where he slipped out of his clothes and pulled on a pair of light pajamas. With two kids, he had learned some time ago to wear something to bed, just in case. Then he brushed his teeth and slipped between the sheets.

"Marky, I miss you," he said quietly into the darkness.

Over the past fifteen months, he had stopped listening for a reply, though he still wished for one. It was stupid, and he knew that. Mark wasn't coming back. A snowy late-night car accident on his way home from work at one of the warehouses outside Carlisle had resulted in Mark's car exploding. So after three years and two kids, Willy had found himself alone again. At first Grant had asked where Papa was, but over time, he had stopped. Willy was pretty sure that he was the only one in their apartment who remembered him now, though there were pictures, with one hanging in the kids' room. He liked to think of Mark watching over them.

He hated that he was getting maudlin again. Pushing away the sense of loss as best he could, Willy rolled over and closed his eyes. He had to get the kids up, fed, and to the Dickinson College daycare before eight, so his day started early, with his first class beginning at nine. Thankfully it didn't take long before fatigue set in and sleep overtook him.

WILLY DREAMED that he couldn't find his way out of the fog. He had had the dream before, and he always found himself in a cloud bank and could never get out. He could see nothing, yet somehow he knew that there was a cliff, and all it would take was one wrong step and he'd fall into oblivion. Only this time it was worse, because he kept coughing. Maybe this wasn't fog, but smoke. That would teach him to watch a movie with fire-breathing dragons before going to bed.

He coughed again, realizing he wasn't totally asleep. Sitting up in bed, he reached for the light next to him, but nothing happened. The room was dark, with only the light from outside coming in. He coughed hard, realizing the smoke was real.

Fire. There was a fire. Willy rolled out of bed and onto the floor. It was a little better there. He crawled to the door and out into the hall, where it was worse. A crash somewhere in the building made him move faster. He opened the door to the kids' room and closed it again behind him. There wasn't much smoke in there.

He lifted April out of her crib, and she went right into his arms. "Grant, wake up," he said firmly. "We need to get out." He heard the rising panic in his voice.

"Daddy." Grant rubbed his eyes.

"Stand up on the bed," Willy said, and once Grant did that, he grabbed Grant's blanket and handed it to him. "Put this over your head," he told him before lifting Grant into his arms. "Put it over April's too." She cried, but Grant did as he told him. "Now, both of you hold tight to me. I'm going to get us out of here." He opened the bedroom door and hurried out through the smoky apartment and into the hall. They were on the second of three floors.

His ears rang, and all Willy could think was that he had to get the three of them out of here. "Jesus Christ," he breathed when he looked up to where flames had engulfed the ceiling above him. Without thinking, he headed for the stairs and made it to the bottom. He turned and ran for the front door, but his legs gave out, and he went to his knees, still holding the kids. Whatever happened to him didn't matter, but he had to get the kids out.

"Daddy," Grant cried as April coughed. But Willy's head spun as he tried to get up. All he needed was to make it to the door, but moving was nearly impossible. Still, he tried again to get to his feet and managed to stand. The door was just a few feet away, and yet it seemed like a mile. Maybe he wasn't going to make it after all and he'd see Marky much sooner than he thought.

THE WEIGHT in his arms lifted, and it was just him. Willy could barely remember a thing, but the kids were gone. He tried to reach for them, but he couldn't find them. "It's okay," a deep, gruff voice said. "They're fine."

Willy inhaled and then coughed, but he managed to breathe once more and realized the air was clear, even if his lungs felt like they were filled with gunk.

"Just relax. I'm taking you to the ambulance, and they'll help you."

"Taking me," Willy mumbled and coughed again. Somehow he managed to open his eyes, and then he found himself pressed tightly to a firefighter's chest as he was carried across the parking lot in front of his building. "Are you for real? Did I die and go to hunky fireman heaven?"

He received a chuckle. "No. You're alive."

"Though the hunky fireman part is real," a female voice said. "Kevin, put him right here and I'll check him over."

Kevin—the hunky fireman was Kevin. Somehow Willy's brain processed that as he was gently laid down. A mask was placed on his face, and it got easier to breathe.

"Stay calm and just breathe. Let's get some good air in your lungs."

"My kids," Willy said.

"They're with my partner, but they're doing well. You got the worst of it. Just relax," she told him, but Willy couldn't. All he could think about was them.

A crash made him jump, but the woman put her hand on his arm to calm him. It took Willy a moment to realize the sound had been part of the building they lived in crashing to the ground. He kept his eyes closed and tried not to think about the fact that the three of them were homeless.

"Do you hurt anywhere other than your lungs?"

"Knees," Willy said.

"Can you lift your legs and bend your knees?" He tried, and they worked. "Is the pain sharp or sore?"

"Sore, I guess," he managed to answer. Maybe that meant he hadn't broken anything.

"Good," she said. "Now just stay there. I'll be right back." He closed his eyes and tried to block out the sound around him. "I have someone for you." She placed April into his arms, and Willy soothed her gently. At least she was okay, judging by her cries, which settled once he could hold her.

"Sweet girl. It's okay. You're with me now." He cradled her, and her crying softened.

"Daddy, are you dead like Papa?" Grant asked from next to him, and Willy took his hand.

"None of us are dead," he told him.

"We're going to take all of you to the hospital," the woman EMT told him. "We just want them to check you out to make sure you're okay."

"What about everyone else? Did they get out?" Willy asked, turning to look at her.

She smiled. "I believe so." That was a relief. She called someone over. "This is Kevin."

Willy smiled up into the rugged face that filled his vision. "Thank you for finding us," he said quietly. "You saved my family." He wanted to cry right there. April had settled next to him, and he held Grant's hand, turning to where he'd stuck the thumb of his other hand in his mouth. Grant hadn't done that in months. They were all stressed to the gills, and Willy knew it was about to get worse. The building they had lived in was gone, along with everything they owned except maybe the car.

"I'm just glad I could help."

Grant pulled his thumb out of his mouth. "Are you a real fireman?"

"Yes, I am. I found you and your sister and daddy and helped you get out, though your daddy did the hard work. He got you down by the door. He was very brave."

Willy didn't feel brave. All he wanted to do was close his eyes and figure out a way to escape the mess their lives were sure to become.

"Let's get all of you in the ambulance," the EMT said. "You too," she told the fireman. "I want you checked out as well. You spent a lot of time in the smoke." Willy watched as Kevin was about to protest, but he shrugged in the end.

They loaded Willy in the back with April still in his arms. Kevin held out his hand, and Grant took it. Then he lifted Grant inside and took a seat, with Grant buckled in the one next to him. The space was cramped, but they all got inside with the EMT right next to Willy, and soon the siren sounded as they began to move.

"I'm feeling better," Willy said.

"That's good. Just keep the oxygen on for a while. It will ease any stress on your lungs. And it's okay to cough. That helps to bring up the particles you inhaled." She sat quietly while Kevin answered a million of Grant's questions. It seemed that once he knew that Willy was going to be okay, his natural curiosity went into overdrive. Willy smiled as Kevin patiently spoke with him.

"Do you get hot in all that?" Grant asked.

"Yes, sometimes. But the gear keeps me from getting burned, and it keeps the water out." Kevin sounded so interested. Grant tended to wear people out with his questions.

"Do you wear pants under there too?" Grant asked.

"I wear shorts," Kevin answered as though he were sharing a secret. "Maybe after this is over and all of you are okay, you can come down to the fire station and I'll show you everything."

"Even the siren and the dog?" Grant said, clearly in a bit of awe.

"Dog?"

"In books, firehouses always have Dalmatians," Willy supplied. "We have a story about a fire dog." Or at least they used to. "And it's one of his favorites." He closed his eyes and tried not to let the darkness that threatened wash over him. Willy wished his mind would clear, but it seemed determined to go in circles, and that wasn't helping with anything.

They were all on their way to the hospital, and that meant that for the next few hours, the three of them would be taken care of. Willy was a planner—he liked to try to schedule weeks and months in the future— but an accident like this reminded him just how easily everything could be taken away. And when that happened, looking hours ahead seemed good enough.

"Just relax. We're almost there," the EMT told him, and Willy sighed and closed his eyes once more. The burning in his lungs had already subsided, as had the constant need to cough. April had fallen asleep in his arms, and Grant was talking a mile a minute with Kevin. So at least for the moment, things were the best he could hope for.

Of course everything changed when they reached the ER. It was loud and bright, and once they had Willy in a room, Grant decided that he wanted to be in the bed with Daddy, which made April fuss. The nurse managed to get an IV into Willy's arm, and he squeezed into the bed with Grant on one side and April on the other. He had no room to move, but at least the kids were quiet… until they weren't.

"How are you doing?" Kevin asked a little while later, standing in the doorway. "Gosh, are you squashed?"

"A little." He was wiped out and only wanted to close his eyes for a while. The doctor had said that he wanted to run some tests, so they had been waiting.

"Here. Let me hold her," Kevin said, gently lifting April into his arms before sitting in the chair next to the bed. He said soft things to her as he held her. April seemed content as she curled her hands around Kevin's neck.

"You must have the magic touch, because she won't let anyone but me hold her when she's tired. At least not since we lost Mark. She was very much his little girl." God, Willy would have loved for Mark to have seen how they'd grown.

"I guess I do. My sister and brother-in-law have twins about her age, and after they were born, I spent time with them, helping out. They boys always went to sleep so easy for me."

Willy could see that. "I guess I should introduce myself since you're holding my daughter. William Daugherty."

"Kevin Messier," the firefighter told him with a gentle smile.

"And you're holding April, and this is Grant." He shared the smile as the nurse came in and took some blood for testing.

"Your blood oxygen levels are looking good." She listened to his chest. "And your lungs are clear, which is even better. The doctor ordered a few more tests, and then you'll all be able to go home."

Willy clamped his eyes closed. Tests could take hours, and they had already been waiting much of the night.

"They were caught in that fire tonight. There isn't a home to go back to," Kevin told her quietly. "I contacted the Red Cross emergency number on their behalf, and they said that they would be sending someone over. Is there a way to let the front desk people know? It's early enough that people should be starting to come in."

"Of course," the nurse said. She left the room, and Willy relaxed a little. The Red Cross wasn't going to let him down, or at least he hoped not. All he needed was a place to stay for a few days so he could get in touch with his insurance company and hopefully find a place that was immediately available. That was all he could hope for.

Kevin shifted April to his other shoulder, talking to her quietly as he did. Then he pulled out his phone and made a call. "Chase, I need a favor. Do you know any landlords in the area who might have a place available?" he asked. "Yeah… for one of those families. A guy with two young kids." He went quiet, and Willy appreciated the effort no matter how it turned out. "Thanks. Is it too early to call? Cool. Text me the number." He ended the call, and his phone dinged. He made another call. "Ellen, hello. I was given your number by Chase at the fire station. He said you might have a place to rent out." He listened. "I'll let you talk to Willy. Hold on." Then Kevin handed him the phone, and Willy was grateful they had shifted him from a mask to a nasal canula for the oxygen.

"Hello. I'm William Daugherty. Our building over by the Giant was destroyed in a fire, and I need a place to live for me and my two kids. I'm a professor of economics at Dickinson."

"Willy, it's Ellen Thompson. We met last year at the arts benefit," she explained. Willy breathed a sigh of relief. "George and I were just finishing up cleaning and painting at the unit on South and West. It's ground floor, with three bedrooms. I was just about to list it, but it's yours if you want it."

"Oh, thank God," he breathed. "I'm at the hospital with the kids, but they're going to let us go soon. We have nothing but the clothes we're wearing. Everything else apparently burned with the building."

"George and I can rustle up a few beds and maybe a sofa and stuff. I'll see what we have. Why don't we meet tomorrow afternoon and you can look the place over and we can take it from there?" She sounded so upbeat that Willy felt hopeful for the first time since they'd almost… well, he didn't want to think about that.

"Thank you," Willy said and handed Kevin back his phone. "She has a place for us." He slowly sat up and breathed deeply, grateful he didn't cough.

"It's not a problem. You'll need a place to stay for tonight, so if you want, you and the kids can come home with me. It will be for a day or two, but with the car show going on, every hotel is booked solid."

"Are you sure? You don't know us from Adam." Willy thought he was going to cry. No one had been this kind to him since Mark passed away, and he wasn't sure how to handle it.

"It's no problem. These two need a place to sleep, and you can start to pick up the pieces in the morning." Kevin gently patted Willy's shoulder, and he sighed at the kindness of strangers. Maybe there was a way forward after all.

CHAPTER 2

WHAT ELSE was he supposed to do? He had April in his arms, and the little girl seemed so content. Kevin loved kids. They were without guile and didn't hold things back. Secrets were foreign to them, at least at this age, and Kevin had had enough secrets for an entire lifetime. He knew every hotel in town was booked solid and had been for months. They always were on car show weekends. It was part of the summer life blood that kept the town going, but it made situations like this even harder.

"Are you sure?" Willy asked. "I'm certain the Red Cross will be able to find somewhere for us."

"Yes. They have an emergency shelter in their building downtown. It's an open room on the second floor with cots and a few lockers. That's about it. They'll put the three of you up there for the night, along with everyone else they are caring for at the moment. I'm sure of it. But that isn't what you need." He knew what those places were like. He and his mother had been homeless for a year after his father had left them, and he'd spent much of that time in shelters or living in a tent in the back of the park. The tent had been pretty cool until they were forced to leave. Then it was back to the shelters and rooms full of people. Kevin swore he didn't sleep for months—not until Mom managed to get a job, with some help, and then a small apartment that one of the churches helped with the rent for a year. But it got them back on their feet.

"I see."

"So like I said, you can stay with me for a few nights until you can get some things together and move into the new apartment. But I suppose I should make sure no one is allergic or scared of dogs." Willy shook his head, and Kevin leaned a little closer to the bed. "Don't worry about everything all at once. Just take things one step at a time. You have a place to go in a day or so. You and the kids are safe."

Willy nodded slowly. "Do you think we will be able to see if anything survived the fire?"

Kevin shook his head. "The building is nothing but a burned-out shell. The outside walls are all that is left standing. Everything on the inside burned away to nothing. There might be some remains in the basement, but that's about all." He hated giving him that news. It felt like stripping away Willy's hope.

"My phone and wallet were still inside."

"We can get you a new phone tomorrow, and you can call to replace your credit cards and go to the driver's license center to get a new one. Just one thing at a time." He sat back, trying to stay level-headed for Willy and the kids.

The doctor came into the room and smiled. "It looks like everyone is camped out in here." He checked his chart. "Your blood work came back pretty good. You need to take it easy for a few days. You inhaled a lot of smoke, and it will take time for your lungs to get rid of it. But your blood oxygen levels are good, and they're remaining steady."

"So no marathons in my near future?" Willy said with a smile.

"Exactly. Watch anything strenuous for the next week or so, and remember to give your lungs a chance to heal." The doctor turned to Kevin. "I'd tell you the same thing, but you won't listen."

"I didn't get much, and I had breathing gear. I'm fine." Kevin stayed where he was, still holding April, who was fast asleep. "But thank you for everything."

"There's a woman here from the Red Cross. I'm going to discharge all four of you, and I'll get that going while you talk to her." He left, and a middle-aged woman with kind eyes and a gentle smile came inside.

"I'm Berry Silver, and I'm sorry about what happened," she said softly. "And it's early and you've had a long night, so I'll get to the point."

Kevin interrupted her. "I think I can save you some time. Willy and the kids are going to stay with me for a few days. They have an appointment tomorrow to look at a place that a friend has available. But other than that, they lost everything."

Her eyes widened. "That's very kind. I have care kits in the car for you and each of the kids. There are basic toiletries and some supplies. They also have activity books for them, things like that." She checked her clipboard. "I was told that your daughter is two and a half and that your son is five."

"He's four," Willy corrected.

She nodded. "Based on what I had, I brought a basic change of clothes for them. They may be a little big."

Willy sniffed. "Thank you."

"I also have a gift card from Target. You can use it to get additional clothes for the three of you." She reached into her bag and pulled out a pair of teddy bears. She handed one to Willy, who placed it near Grant. He must have sensed it was there, because he cuddled it right up to him and slept on. The other she handed to Kevin, and he held on to it for April. These kids were going to need all the comfort they could get in the next few days.

"Thank you for everything."

"I'll go get the kits and bring them in for you." She left, and Kevin shifted April to his other arm. She woke at that, blinking her big eyes.

"Hi, sweetheart. I'm Kevin," he said softly. "Your daddy is right over there." He turned her so she could see him. "Did you sleep well?" He showed her the bear, and she grabbed it, hugging it to her. Then she sniffled. "Are you thirsty?" Kevin asked, and she nodded. "Do you like milkshakes?"

"Donald?" she asked.

"From McDonald's? Yes. She likes them."

"Then let's get them ready to go. Let me call one of the guys to come pick us all up. My car is still at the station." Kevin called the captain and explained what he needed.

"I'll send Ralph. He has that kidmobile of his, complete with car seats. He can get you all home."

"Thanks," Kevin said.

Once the papers were signed, April let him carry her out, so he had her on one side and a bag of things from the Red Cross in his other hand. He felt like a bit of a pack mule. Ralph pulled up a few minutes later, and they got everyone and everything loaded in the van and took off for his row house on West South Street, but not before going through the drive-through for shakes and fries for all of them. Comfort food it was.

They pulled into the drive area and got everyone out. The house had been built on a double lot, so it had a drive alongside it as well as a larger fenced-in yard. "Let's go inside, but be careful, okay?" He unlocked the door and pushed it back gently before going inside. The three dogs all crowded around for pets. "This is Thumper, Benjamin, and Elsa. They're all nice dogs." Kevin had rescued them. Elsa he'd found at the scene of a fire at an abandoned house. She was a bulldog mix with short red hair and was the calm one and a real sweetheart. Benjamin was a terrier mix and had all the energy in the world, but was sweet and loved attention. Kevin had found him huddled in the basement after a house fire, and no one had claimed him. Thumper was the oldest, and Kevin had gotten him at a shelter when he was a puppy.

April squirmed to get down, and as soon as he set her on her feet, the dogs swarmed her. She laughed and petted each of them like they were there just for her. Grant stayed in Willy's arms for a few minutes before joining her, the dogs soaking up the attention.

"Come on. We need to get both of you a quick breakfast and then down for a rest," Willy said, and Kevin led the way to the kitchen, where he made some toast with jam. The kids ate, half asleep, and then he took them upstairs, with Willy and the pack following.

"I don't have a crib for April," Kevin said, realizing she might still need one.

"She's fine in a regular bed. Once she goes to sleep, she stays pretty still." Willy yawned and set about getting the kids out of their smoky clothes. The Red Cross had provided a nightgown with a princess on it for April, and she went right down to sleep in one of the twin beds. Willy got Grant into pajamas that were a little too big, but had dinosaurs on them that he seemed to like. He climbed into the other bed, both kids hugging the bears.

"Kids are resilient," Kevin said as Benjamin jumped onto April's bed and curled up between her and the edge, while Elsa claimed the foot of Grant's. Thumper seemed left out, but both dogs gave him the stink eye as he looked over each bed, so he left the room. "They'll be fine. All the dogs are good with kids."

Willy nodded and followed him out of the room and across the hall to the room where his sister and brother-in-law stayed when they came to town. "This is really nice," Willy said, sitting on the edge of the bed before covering his mouth and coughing deeply. He was still in the pajamas, now covered with ash and the scent of smoke, that Kevin had found him in.

"Let me get you something to wear." Kevin left the room and found a pair of sweatpants that he was planning to donate because they were too small. He also grabbed a T-shirt and brought them to Willy. "Get some rest, and you can take care of things after you sleep."

"Thank you for everything," Willy said softly, holding the clothes that Kevin had given him in his lap. "I don't know what I'd be doing without you." He shivered, and Kevin smiled at him and drew the door partway closed. Thumper followed him back to his room and jumped onto the bed, making himself comfortable as Kevin used the bathroom to clean up and then returned to his room, slipping under the covers in his boxers and then turning off the light.

He listened. The house was so quiet, yet he found himself straining to hear any noise that seemed out of place. He wasn't used to having strangers in the house, and he found himself a little on edge in case they needed something. Still, the house stayed quiet, and eventually Kevin fell asleep, but he woke to movement somewhere.

He got out of the bed and quietly left his room in time to see Willy leaving the kids' room and closing the door. "Is everything okay?" he whispered.

"Yes. Each of the kids has a dog watching over them." Kevin turned toward him, and Willy stopped. "Umm…," he stammered for a second. "Sorry, I should get back to bed." He hurried into the bedroom and closed the door. Kevin wondered what had happened until he looked down and realized he had on just his boxers. Kevin smiled to himself and went back to bed.

He woke alone after a few hours, which was unusual. He usually had a dog curled on the bed with him, but not this morning. Sounds drifted in from elsewhere in the house, something that sounded like singing. He got up and pulled on shorts and a T-shirt before leaving the room. The other bedrooms were empty, so he followed the sound downstairs to where Willy had Grant sitting at the table and April on his lap, the kids eating slices of apple. All three dogs sat nearby, watching in case anything fell to the floor.

"I didn't mean to wake you," Willy said. "They were hungry. I hope it's okay if I gave them some apple."

"Get whatever you need," Kevin said. "Is the apple good?" he added to the kids, who both nodded. A piece of April's dropped on the floor, and Elsa got there first. April giggled and grabbed another piece of apple, looking toward the floor.

"No, little miss. You eat it." Willy was gentle with her. "Mr. Kevin is going to feed the dogs properly. The apple is for your tummy."

"I could make some toast and scrambled eggs," Kevin offered.

"Eggies!" Grant cheered, and Kevin took that as a yes. He got out the pans and whipped up a batch of light and fluffy eggs, then popped some bread in the toaster. Then he found some plates and brought them to the table. Willy helped the kids with their food and ate some of the eggs himself.

"Is it good?" Kevin asked as he sat down with his own breakfast.

"Yummy," Grant reported as he shoveled in the eggs. Apparently they were a big hit with him. April was more interested in the toast, which was fine considering she kept giving her eggs to the dogs, like it was some kind of game.

"I need to get my car, and we should arrange to get yours as well. The station is only a few blocks away, so I figured I'd walk over to get it. Then we can check on yours, and I'll take you to the driver's license center and to get a phone."

"I'm off today. Do you need to work?" Thank goodness for Sunday.

"No. It's my day off too."

"I don't have anything to prove who I am."

"We'll figure it out. They have to have a picture from your old license and should be able to look it up to verify your identity." God, he hoped that would be good enough. He finished his breakfast and helped Grant with his. Once they were all done, Willy took the kids upstairs to clean up while Kevin put the dishes in the dishwasher.

It took fifteen minutes for him to get to the station and get his car. By the time he returned, Willy had the kids dressed and ready to go. "We should get my car first. It has the car seats in it. Then we can do the rest of the running and stuff."

"Good idea," Kevin told him, and they rode over to the building in silence, with Willy growing quieter the closer they got. Kevin pulled up to the burned-out shell, and Willy gasped. There really was very little left of the building itself. The decorative gable at the top now curved forward like the curl of a melting candle.

"Oh God," Willy breathed. "We were inside there."

"Hey. Everyone got out. A few others were sent to the hospital, but everyone is going to be okay." Kevin tried to be soothing. "Where is your car parked?" Willy pointed to the Volvo sedan. "And the keys?" he asked. Willy pulled the set out of his pocket. "I grabbed them on my way out. They were in a bowl on the table near the door, and I just grabbed them out of habit, I guess." He unlocked the doors, and Kevin helped him get the kids transferred over. "Do you want to ride with us?"

"Follow me back to the house, and I'll leave my car there." Kevin led the way through town and got in the passenger seat once he'd parked his car. "Maybe I should drive. I'm the one with a license right now." They switched places, and Kevin took Willy out to the center.

"You need some form of ID," the woman at the counter told them.

"Ma'am," Kevin said levelly, "he lost everything in a fire." He pulled out his phone. "See, this is what's left. He needs a replacement license. There has to be a way to help him."

Fortunately, a supervisor overheard them and came over. Willy explained everything again. Then he provided all his information. "If you look it up, you'll see it's my picture. I just need a replacement." He was getting frustrated, but the supervisor seemed to know what to do, and after he'd filled out forms and the supervisor verified his signature and picture, Willy walked out with a new license. At least that was one victory. The next was the phone store, which took less time, and finally Willy was able to contact his insurance company and file a total-loss claim. What a pain in the butt, though the pictures Willy was able to supply seemed to get the point across.

"Daddy, I'm hungry," Grant said, and Willy took them all to Red Robin for burgers, using his phone to pay the bill, before heading to Target for a set of clothes for each of them.

"I feel like I'm trying to put all the pieces of my life back together and I don't know what the picture is supposed to look like."

"It'll look like whatever you want it to," Kevin said.

Willy seemed to take it in as he pushed the cart with April in the seat and Grant holding his daddy's hand. They were an adorable family, something Kevin had always wanted. His ex, Masten, hadn't wanted children. It had taken Kevin time to realize that he was just too selfish to have anyone take away any sort of attention from him. But Kevin had always wanted a family of his own. He pulled himself out of the daydream and back to reality. This was Willy's family, and he was just helping them out, nothing more. He needed to remember that they would move into their own place and go on with their lives, just like he would.

CHAPTER 3

"THIS IS great, Ellen," Willy said as he walked through the empty space. It was the entire first floor and had three bedrooms. There was only one bath, but that was okay. It was bigger than their old place, and the kitchen was larger. The appliances had been updated, so while they weren't fancy, they were new, and he wasn't going to be dealing with an oven that had eighty years of crap baked on inside it.

"There's also a backyard. It isn't huge, but that comes with this unit as well. You have the only door that gets out to it."

"Would it be all right if I got a play structure for the kids? It wouldn't be huge, but…."

Ellen smiled. "Go ahead. You could put it right over there under the shade of the maple if you wanted."

In so many ways, this was a better place than the one they'd had. There was more space, and the price Ellen had quoted was about the same as what he had been paying, so it wasn't going to stretch his budget.

"I took a look up in the attic at the store, and we found three bed frames. They're a little banged up, but serviceable. We'll bring them over in the next day or so. You'll need mattresses and things, but at least you'll have the frames. There's also a few tables and other items. I know it isn't much, but it might help."

Willy didn't know what to say. "Thanks. Right now I don't have anything. I'll stop at the bank and get a check for the deposit and stuff and deliver it." This really was a godsend for all of them. At least with a place to live, they could start to put the pieces of their lives back together. "Kevin has been kind enough to let us stay with him." He smiled over to where the man in question held an exhausted April on his shoulder and spoke with Grant. The guy was gorgeous, that was for certain, and Willy had definitely gotten a good look at him last night. Seeing him standing in the hallway in nothing but a pair of boxers, Willy had been torn between embarrassment and sheer attraction. Part of him had wanted to jump the guy right there, but even if Kevin liked guys, what would he see in a skinny professor father like him? Still, that sight was something he would hold on to for quite a while. After all, it wasn't every day that you got to see a sexy fireman in next to nothing.

"I'm glad someone was able to help," Ellen said. "I brought the lease agreement with me. Just review and sign it. Then return it when you bring the check and we'll be all set." She handed Willy the keys. "I really hope you and the kids will be happy here."

"I really think so," Willy told her. The timing couldn't have been better.

"Daddy," Grant said as he raced over, "Mr. Kevin says that I get my own room here."

"Yes, you do, and so does April. I'll have my own room too." Grant jumped up and down, clearly excited. "I think you're really going to like it here. Mrs. Ellen says there's a park not too far away, and there's also a backyard for you and April to play in."

"Can I get a bike?" Grant asked.

"Maybe." It was good to see that the loss of their home hadn't scarred the kids too much. It probably hurt Willy more than them. "Say thank you to Mrs. Ellen for helping us find a new place to live."

"Thank you. I love it," Grant said, and Ellen grinned, tousling Grant's hair as she headed for the door.

"Let me know if you need anything," Ellen said and left, leaving Willy and the kids to what was to become their new family home.

April had woken up fussy, so Kevin suggested they head back to the house. It was only half a block, so they walked to Kevin's. "I can't thank you enough for how kind you've been to us. We'll be out of your hair soon. I promise."

Kevin stopped on the sidewalk. "You haven't been any trouble. I've liked having you. The house seems empty most of the time, and you all filled it." Their gazes met for just a moment, and Willy was surprised at the heat that simmered behind Kevin's eyes. He licked his lips and felt completely stupid for letting himself think that Kevin had any interest in him other than as someone who needed help. Still, Kevin didn't look away until Grant whined softly that he was hungry.

"Then let's get you to the house. What does your tummy want?" Kevin asked.

"A cookie," Grant answered without skipping a beat.

"I don't think I have any of those, but we'll look and see if your tummy will be happy with something else." He scooped Grant up, and

Grant giggled as Kevin flew him around and down the sidewalk. April squirmed, so Willy flew her around too. The happy laughter touched his heart, and some of the gloom that seemed to hang over him lifted like fog in the sun.

"Do you like being an airplane?" Kevin asked, and both kids giggled as they soared over the sidewalk.

Once they were inside, Willy and Kevin got the kids at the table with some fruit, the dogs in their places hoping for anything that might drop to the floor. Kevin sat down next to him with an apple and a knife. After a minute, he lightly bumped Willy's shoulder, offering him a piece. Willy took it and bit into the crisp apple as Kevin's phone rang.

He pulled it out of his pocket and checked the number before answering. "Captain?" He grew silent and then stood and left the table.

"Is Kevin going to live with us?" Grant asked.

"No. Kevin lives here, and we're only staying with him for a few days. But the three of us will move into the apartment we saw today. You'll have your own room, and soon I'll be able to get you some new toys." God, he hoped that the insurance came through.

"Oh," Grant said before eating some more apple. Willy sat with the kids and waited for Kevin to return, which he did after a few minutes.

"I need to go for a while. Help yourself to anything in the refrigerator or the pantry for dinner." He grabbed a bag of gear that sat near the back door and hurried out.

"Where's he going?" Grant asked.

"Someone needs his help the way we did," Willy said as Kevin paused in the doorway for a second before turning to give him a smile and then racing off. "Be safe," he added, even though the door had already closed behind him.

"I MADE up a plate for you," Willy said softly when Kevin came home hours later. Kevin was dirty and covered in soot. He smelled like fire. "Are you okay?" he asked when Kevin just stared at him blankly. "What happened?"

Kevin dropped his bag with a thunk, and Willy hurried over to help him into a chair. "I wasn't supposed to be at a fire, but…." He placed his hands on the table and didn't move otherwise.

Willy sat next to him, the scent of fire taking him back to the smoke-filled hallway, but he pushed that away. He could flashback later. Right now, Kevin needed someone to listen.

"A call came in while we were investigating the fire at your old building." He closed his eyes. "The house was pretty bad already when I got there. They said there was someone still inside, but it was too dangerous to try to enter. I tried through one of the side windows and managed to get into the next bedroom, but the floor gave way and I had to get right back out."

"I see. Someone died," Willy said softly, and Kevin nodded.

"I'll be okay. This is one of the hardest parts of the job. Sometimes you make it in time, but sometimes…." His voice trailed off. "The worst part is when you lose a child."

"Is that what happened?"

"This time it was the grandmother. She was bedridden. The family tried to get her out, but they couldn't." He lowered his head, and Willy stood and hugged him. Kevin wound his arms around Willy's waist and hugged him back. They stood at the kitchen table without saying a word, simply holding one another.

"You did everything you could," Willy said softly before inhaling. Kevin smelled like smoke, but there was something earthy and rich underneath that he wanted more of.

Kevin turned around. "How do you know? How *could* you know?"

"Because of what you did for me… and the kids. I have no doubt that if there was any way to reach this person, you would have found it." He backed away and got the plate he'd put together out of the refrigerator. He put it in the microwave to heat before getting Kevin a beer and setting a place for him. Once the food was ready, he set the plate in front of him and then sat down.

"In my head, I know this can happen, but when it actually does…." Kevin sighed, and Willy sat with him while he ate. Once he was done, he took the plate to the sink and brought over a plastic container, opened it, and set it on the table.

"The kids wanted to make you cookies since you had to work." Willy took out one of the misshapen chocolate chip cookies and handed it to Kevin. "Grant was the one to put them on the tray." They were all over the place, but they tasted good.

"Thank you." He sat back and ate the cookie before taking another one. "The call I got wasn't because of the fire. The captain wanted me to meet one of the other guys at your old building."

"Do they know what caused the fire?"

"We believe it started in one of the lower unit kitchens. Probably electrical. But that's only part of the problem. From what we can piece together, the fire spread from one unit to the other in minutes. It was less than fifteen before the entire building was engulfed. That's way too fast, and we need to know why."

"Everyone got out, though," Willy said, a little confused.

"Yes, and that was a miracle, since some of the smoke alarms don't appear to have been working. Yours weren't, were they? You told me you woke because of the smoke, not from an alarm."

He was shocked. It hadn't even occurred to him. "You're right. The kids were asleep, and they would have been awake if a smoke alarm had gone off. So you think something was wrong?"

"We're not sure yet. But we're going to have to check the other buildings in the complex to see if they have any issues. The fire marshal's office has the right to inspect locations like this, especially after a fire, so that isn't the issue. We just have to go through proper channels."

"The walls in that place were always so thin. I had to be careful how loudly I watched the TV at night for fear I'd wake the kids, and they were in another room with the door closed. I swear it was like the walls weren't there. And I can't tell you how many times the people in one of the other units burned their dinner and we could smell it."

"That shouldn't happen. The units should each be vented separately. What else can you tell me about that place?"

"Like what?"

"It was built fifteen years ago. Did it have GFI outlets?"

"Yeah, but they didn't do anything."

"Could you hear your neighbors?" Kevin asked.

Willy scoffed. "All the time. Especially the people below us if they watched television loudly. One of the units had a Christmas party, and I couldn't put the kids to bed until nearly midnight because it was too loud and they refused to sleep. I mean, I know that places like that are built quickly, but…."

Kevin looked up from where he'd been making notes. "None of that should happen. I'm going to need to go to the borough office and pull the plans for that building, see how it was built, because that shouldn't be." He set his notes aside. "Are you familiar with that sort of thing?"

"Not really. But if someone explains what we're looking at, I should be able to tell if it was there or not. At least some things." He would be happy to try to help. "I suppose a lot of the evidence burned up in the fire."

"Yeah, it would have, especially with how hot and fast the building went up. From what I saw today in the few minutes I was there, the basement is filled with debris, ash, and charred wood. The entire contents of the building are now a giant heap, with most of the interior walls and floors gone. I'm surprised that the side walls are still standing. Though if we get a wind storm, they could collapse."

"I suppose that's why you aren't digging through what's left." Willy put the cookies away. "It makes sense, for safety's sake." He cleared away the rest of the dishes and put them in the dishwasher. "Why don't you go on upstairs and take a shower? The kids are asleep, so be quiet. I would have closed their doors, but each of them has a dog in bed with them."

"You can call them out if you feel you need to."

Willy shook his head. "April has her bear in one arm and the other on Benjamin, and he's curled between her and the edge of the bed. Elsa is with Grant. I think the dogs soothe them, and right now, I'm grateful for anything that makes them happy." He wasn't sure what he was going to do when they were in their new apartment; he'd just have to take things one day at a time. "Last night, Thumper here spent part of the time with me. It was nice knowing I wasn't alone." He left the room, needing a few seconds to himself to get his feelings under control. They were too close to the surface, and Kevin did not need to see that. He turned on the television and tried not to pay attention, and Kevin went upstairs.

When Kevin returned, he sat on the sofa near him. "I know this has been hard for you, but I get the feeling there's more going on than you're talking about. It's like you're going through the motions, but that's all."

"What else am I supposed to do? I'm not keeping secrets. But I keep thinking how close we all came to dying. I tried to get the kids out of that building, but what if I had been a little later, or if you hadn't been there to get us? A few more minutes and all that fire would have come down on us." His little family would have been gone.

Kevin nodded slowly and put an arm around him. "I understand how you feel."

"I know you do because of what happened today. But that only brought home how close we all came to the end. And I'm frightened. What if we move into the new place and something happens? What if I can't get to the kids? What if I hadn't been able to?" His entire mind seemed on this loop that wouldn't shut off, and he didn't know what to do.

"Okay, first thing, you look a little wild, so close your eyes and take a deep breath, hold it for a few seconds, and then let it out slowly." Kevin's voice was so calm that Willy did as he asked and then did it again. "Let go of all the things that could have happened and think about what did. You got to the kids and tried to get them out of the building. You could have made it out yourself very easily, but April and Grant were more important. The three of you are safe because of what you did. I was coming in to try to find all of you, and there you were right inside the door. I got you all out and away from the building. So you're all safe because of what you did." He took Willy's hand. "And as for the new place, we are going to make sure that there is a working smoke alarm in every room, fire extinguishers, and that the wiring is done properly. You are all on the first floor, so we'll also make sure all the windows open and that you know how to get out if you can't reach the front door."

Willy's panic attack seemed to be abating. "I know we can't stop everything."

"No, but we can make sure that you know what to do. Now, it's unlikely that anything is going to happen, so remember that you and the kids are safe, and that's what matters. All the worry about what might have happened is wasted energy, and knowing April and Grant for only a few days, I can tell you that you need all the energy you can get." He smiled, and Willy found himself agreeing with him.

Willy was so worn out. He leaned to the side, and Kevin gently tugged him into a hug. Willy went with it, letting himself be pressed against Kevin's hard shoulder and chest. This felt so damned good, like nothing bad could happen as long as he was right here. Slowly, he lifted his head, meeting Kevin's gaze, which grew heated. His heart beat faster, and the room grew warmer as anticipation took hold.

CHAPTER 4

"DADDY, I'M thirsty. Can I have Diet Coke?" Grant asked as he came down the stairs.

Kevin groaned and sat back, trying not to let the disappointment show on his face.

"No. You can have some water," Willy told him and sighed softly as he got up and went to the kitchen. He took the cup of water and Grant back up the stairs and soon loped down them alone.

"Diet Coke?" That was a new one.

"My mother is completely addicted to the stuff. She has it in the house, and whenever they go over to visit, Grant sees it, and she gives him drinks of hers, and now it's his preferred drink if he can get it. I swear by the time he's six, he'll be swilling coffee in the morning, Diet Coke in the afternoon, and trying to take over the world at night." He rolled his eyes and sat back down.

"Did he go back to sleep?" Kevin asked, afraid the moment was gone and that he might have lost his chance. Willy and the kids would be moving into their new place in the next day or so, and he only had so much time in order to make a move. Not that he was sure that Willy wanted him to or that he was ready to move on from the partner he'd lost, but Kevin was pretty sure that he needed to make his intentions known.

God, even in his head it sounded lame.

Willy shrugged. "I have no idea. He rolled over and hugged his bear, and Elsa took her place on his bed like she's guarding his dreams. Those dogs are so sweet. I don't know what the kids are going to do when we leave." They had become attached to them, and Kevin figured he was going to have three very mopey dogs for a few days.

"They're all good pups," Kevin said as he shifted slightly on the sofa. He felt like he was going in for the kill or something, and it just didn't feel right. Instead, he leaned back and closed his eyes.

"When is your next shift?" Willy asked.

"Tomorrow morning," he answered. "I have to be at the station by seven for turnover. I'll come home at some point in the day to let the dogs out and feed them, but I won't be home until late again." He figured by then, Willy would have them in the new apartment. The truth was, he was going to miss having them in the house. It was nice having people fill the space in this old place.

"I thought I'd take the kids to daycare tomorrow. I have a couple classes I need to teach, and then I thought I'd check out some of the secondhand furniture places to see if there was anything that I could use to help furnish the apartment. I don't want the kids to be living in a blank space. I should also see about getting them some toys and books… things like that." He groaned softly. "There's just so much. I wish the insurance company would come through. That would help a lot. But I guess they do things in their own time."

"They do," Kevin agreed and placed his hand on top of Willy's. Their gazes met for a second, and Kevin held still, not wanting to do anything that might break the spell. He leaned closer, and Willy did the same. Then, for a second, he listened for the patter of little feet, just to make sure he wasn't going to get kid-blocked again. "Look, there's something I've wanted to do, but I didn't know if it was what you wanted or if it was the right thing to do. I don't want to push you or make you feel like you have to because you're staying here, but…." Dammit, why in the hell couldn't he shut the hell up? Suddenly he had mouth run-on and sounded like an idiot.

Thankfully, Willy seemed to get the idea, leaning closer and putting him out of his misery by making the first move. His lips were soft and the kiss gentle and sweet. It didn't last long, and Willy backed away with a slight smile on his lips.

"I wanted to do that too, since the other night when you came out in your boxers." He turned beet red and looked away. "You were hot, and I had no idea if you liked me or even liked guys, and there you were in all your hotness just standing there. And instead of saying anything, I ran away like a scared bunny."

"A cute scared bunny," Kevin added. "Look, I meant what I said. I don't want you to feel that…." He swallowed because he had no idea how to say what he wanted to without it sounding bad.

"We can take things slow, okay? I don't know if I can handle anything in the relationship department right now. With the fire and…." He swallowed hard. "Everything. I'm going to need some time and a chance to think things through. I don't do quickies or anything, and I have the kids to think about. Bringing someone into my life also means they're in theirs, so I don't want a revolving door of guys coming and going and breaking their hearts… or my own, for that matter. So let's see what happens, and maybe we can go out once we're a little settled."

Kevin nodded. "Is this taking things too fast?" he asked, moving closer slowly and then sliding his hand around the back of Willy's neck. He waited to see if Willy pulled away and then kissed him. He so wanted another taste of him, and Willy was just as clean and sweet as before. He deepened the kiss slowly, and damn it all if Willy didn't moan deep in his throat.

That little sound was enough to get his motor revved into high gear, but he backed away and ended the kiss, because if he didn't, it was likely he was going to push for things Willy wasn't ready for, though he sure as hell was. Breathing deeply, he sat back and kept his eyes on Willy's. Kevin had made the mistake before of rushing into things. It was usually how he got himself into one of his messes.

"How did you become a firefighter?" Willy asked out of the blue. "I think we need a change of subject." He actually fanned himself. "I can barely think as it is."

"After one kiss?" Kevin asked.

Willy shrugged. "I don't know. I have a tendency to overreact to things like that. It's why I have to go slowly and think stuff over. It would be so easy to let the hormones and the dopamine take over and just jump into bed. It's what a lot of people would do. But I need to think about stuff."

"I get that." Kevin took a few seconds to clear his head. "As for being a fireman, I sort of fell into that… so to speak. I needed a part-time job when I was in high school, and my teacher knew a number of the guys at the fire station near the house. They were looking for someone to do some of the grunt work, and Mr. Evans helped me get the job. I scrubbed the floors and did some painting, stuff like that, for a year or so. Then I asked about further training and volunteering. They said I had to be eighteen to be a full volunteer, but they taught me how all the equipment worked, how to be safe, how to check it all. Soon I was making sure their equipment stayed in good order." He smiled at the memories. There had been a lot of work, but the guys were good to him. "On my eighteenth birthday, I was able to officially train with the firefighters for the first time. We did an exercise, and I came through with flying colors. I got certified after that, and once I finished college, I returned to the station, but they didn't have any openings. The captain at the time made some calls and was able to help me get a job in Mechanicsburg. But eventually I was able to relocate here and come back to town."

"So you trained at the same station you work at now?"

"No. That station is now used for equipment storage. They integrated that station with the one I work at now a few years ago. The station I first worked at was too small for what was really needed, so they built a new one and used the old building to house additional equipment that can be called on when needed."

"I see," Willy said.

"Why did you become a professor?"

Willy grinned. "I loved economics. When I was a freshman in college, economics was the bane of most people's existence, but it just seemed to make sense to me. So I pursued it, and the more I studied, the more I understood how things work together. It was like an entire door opened to me. I just loved it. When I decided to do some graduate work, I chose economics and developed some models that became somewhat predictive of certain types of economic cycles. The funny things is that so much of what economists study is theoretical, so it's lost on a lot of people, and if you ask any economist what he thinks is going to happen, you'll get a different answer from each one of them." A bright light had come on behind Willy's eyes, and his voice held an excitement that Kevin found riveting. And they were talking about economics.

"Which makes it hard to take seriously. I mean, you see it on the internet or on the news and no one knows what to make of it."

"For most people, yes. Everyone wants a definitive answer to a question, not a 'well, it depends' and then a bunch of various possibilities." He shook his head. "Anyway. My work centered on using models to help predict certain real-world effects. If this happens, then this is most likely to happen. And so on. I concentrated on smaller towns and how they can revitalize their economies. I built models and studied successes and failures and came up with a list of recommendations for where they can start."

"And does it work?" Kevin asked.

"It was good enough that the work got me my doctorate and the professorship here at Dickinson. I'm working on some new material at the moment that has the promise of being very interesting. I teach four to five classes a year, and I love it. I teach a freshman class in the fall and a number of higher-level classes during the year. It's fun, and I get a charge out of it. I really do." He sat back, grinning brightly.

"So, I get it now. If I want to get you excited, all I need to do is whisper 'rising GDP leads to growth for all' in your ear and you'll be putty in my hands."

"Kevin…," Willy said, that blush returning. "That was funny. And no. I get excited by economics, but it doesn't get me hot." His cheeks grew even redder. "But you without a shirt on is a different matter."

"It is, huh?" Kevin said with a smirk he hoped was endearing.

"I think I should go on up to bed. I have a big day tomorrow, and you do too." Willy stood and leaned down to kiss him softly. "Good night." Then he scampered out of the room and up the stairs, leaving Kevin to wonder what the hell had just happened. Willy needed to get away from him fast, but he'd kissed him.

Kevin's smile grew huge as he softly called the dogs. All three of them came and followed him to the back door, then went out to do their business before bed. When they came back in, he gave them each a treat. Benjamin and Elsa went right upstairs, and he had little doubt that they were each guarding their kid. Thumper stayed with him, and he gave him scratches and pets before turning out the lights. Then he headed upstairs, cleaned up, and got ready for bed.

Thumper curled up at the end of the bed, and Kevin tried to go to sleep, but images of Willy kept flashing in his mind. The taste of the man was intoxicating, and he replayed their kisses over and over in his head. The house was silent, but Kevin kept listening for movement. It didn't take him long to realize he had been hoping that Willy might join him. But that would have been the antithesis of taking it slow. Kevin rolled over, trying to think of something else, but eventually his restlessness sent Thumper out of the room. Not that he could blame him. Kevin eventually fell asleep, but not until utter exhaustion caught up with him.

"WHAT THE heck is wrong with you?" Chase asked. "You look like you were rode hard and put away wet." He was one of the newer guys in the department and somewhat of a savant on the behavior of fire. More than once he had unraveled a mystery about how or where a fire started.

"I had a rough night," he said flatly. Chase was a good enough guy, but Kevin wasn't going to discuss his sexual frustration with him… or anyone, for that matter. "Any updates on what happened at that apartment fire?"

Chase groaned. "What the fuck *didn't* happen is more the issue. No smoke alarms, and the sprinkler system was clogged. It hadn't been tested in over two years. But still, that doesn't account for how fast the fire spread."

"That's why you and I are heading to the codes office to look at the original plans." He went into the locker area, dropped his gear, and turned back to Chase. "You up for it?"

"Hell yes. I got more questions than *Who Wants To be a Millionaire*." They strode out of the building, and Kevin drove to the borough hall. The codes office knew they were coming and had the plans ready for them.

Kevin looked them over, and so did Chase, but nothing jumped out at them. "These look like everything was done to code. I mean, the plans have everything that's required." He dug deeper into the fire control and suppression plans and found them to be exactly what he would expect.

"But that doesn't mean that the systems were maintained and tested properly," Chase added.

Kevin agreed, but the codes officer showed him where tests had been conducted and had been signed off by the management company. Apparently they had hired an outside firm to test all their buildings within the past year.

"There's no way," Chase told the codes officer. "The fire-suppression system was so gunked up that there was no way it passed any sort of test." He looked determined.

Kevin kept his cool. "Can we get copies of these documents? There is definitely more for us to look into."

Chase fumed as they walked back to the truck.

"Do you think the codes department is complicit in some kind of cover-up?"

Kevin sighed and shook his head. "No, I don't. The complex ran the tests and then gave them the signed paperwork that they filed. What we need is someone who knows what was really going on inside that building, and I think I have that person. Professor Daugherty at Dickinson College was burned out by the fire. He and his kids have been staying with me until they can get in their new place." Even saying the words felt disappointing. He liked having them in the house, and he sure liked seeing Willy every day. But they were going to move on, and once they did, the house would seem empty again and the dogs would wonder what the heck happened. Hell, he was going to miss all of them and he knew it, but wasn't quite ready to admit it.

Chase snickered. "Is that the reason you've been smiling all the time and why you looked like hell this morning? Were you doing the horizontal hula with Daddy?"

Kevin growled. "I've known him for just a few days, and Willy lost his home and almost everything else he had in a fire. He has two kids, and they're all having to deal with a ton of loss and uncertainty…." He left the rest of the thought to hang in the air, and Chase lowered his gaze, which was exactly what he wanted.

"Fine. I was just teasing you a little. Geez, you don't need to bite my head off." He grew quiet for about two seconds. "But I must have hit a nerve. I take it this professor is cute and you like him."

God, this sounded way too much like high school. "Yes. Willy is—well, I'm not going to jump into anything," Kevin admitted, toning down his firm voice. "He says he needs to take things slow, but I don't know what the hell that means."

Chase rolled his eyes. "For God's sake. Do you jump into bed with every guy you meet?" Kevin pulled to a stop at a light and gave Chase a cold stare. "You do. You think that because you look like that, everyone is going fall at your feet or something. You are handsome and built, but—"

"No. It's not like that. It's just I don't know what 'take things slow' means. It's confusing."

"Of course it is. But then again… it's not. If he wants to go slow… then woo him."

"Huh?" Kevin asked.

"Take the guy out. Go on picnics, or find out what he does for fun. If you like Willy, then find out everything there is to know about him… and not in a creepy way. Really get to know him. The bed stuff will come in its own time when you're both ready." Chase rolled his eyes. "Haven't you ever dated anyone before?"

"Yeah, but it was a while ago."

Chase patted his shoulder. "Then you'll figure it out. But really get to know the guy and his kids. Show them that you want to be part of their lives. After all, there's nothing hotter than someone who really cares for you."

CHAPTER 5

"SORRY ABOUT your apartment," Carol said as she left class. Apparently stories about the fire and the fact that Willy had been caught in it were all over the college. Many of his students had said how sorry they were, and a few had asked if he needed anything. It was nice that they cared and made some of the blackness of the loss seem less dire. He headed down the hall and was joined by a colleague.

"Do you have a place to stay?" Evelyn asked as they stopped in the lounge for a cup of coffee. He poured her a mug and got one for himself.

"Yes. After my classes I need to see about some furniture. I also got a message from the insurance company that some money was on the way, which is a big relief."

"Where are you staying now?" she asked as she took the mug he offered her.

"One of the firefighters took us in. He's put me and the kids up for a few days. But I don't want to impose on him, and I really think it's best if we are all able to get on with our lives, you know?" He sipped the coffee and closed his eyes, thinking instantly of Kevin. It would be so easy to get used to having him around. The kids liked him already, and Willy wasn't sure if that was good or not. He didn't want them getting hurt if things didn't work out.

Evelyn's mouth hung open for a second. "So you and the kids are who my nephew took in. I didn't draw the conclusion right away."

"Kevin is your nephew?" Of course they were related. How many Messiers could there be in a town this size? "Then yes. He took us in. Grant and April have already adopted some of his dogs, and I think it's going to be a fight to get them to bed without Elsa and Benjamin after we move into the new place. Your nephew is quite a person. The night of the fire, he rescued the three of us from the building, and then when the Red Cross was running out of space, he offered his extra rooms so the three of us wouldn't end up in a shelter."

"That's Kevin. He was always kind and caring. I was thrilled when he became a firefighter, though my brother tried to worm his way back into Kevin's life and convince him to go to business school and work on Wall Street or some such thing." She shook her head. "Anyone could see that Kevin was a born firefighter."

"He told me the story," Willy said.

"And those dogs…. He rescued each of them in one way or another." She set down her mug and leaned over the table. "Kevin has a huge heart, but his taste in partners is terrible. He dated Delia while he was in college, and man, she was awful."

Willy swallowed. "I see."

Evelyn shrugged. "They lasted about six months. Then he started dating Jeff, which pissed Clair off to no end, but he was no better than her. Jeff was a track star and had to be the center of attention, so whenever Kevin was in the spotlight, Jeff would make a scene or tear him down. It was not a good time."

Willy couldn't help listening and wondered if she should be telling him all this. "Maybe Kevin should be the one to tell me about his past."

"My point is that he has bad taste in the people he dates." She watched him over the mug as she sipped. "I'm wondering if a certain colleague of mine might have captured his interest."

Willy huffed. "I've known Kevin for, what, four days? Don't go playing matchmaker or trying to push us together. Kevin is a good person and he helped us out a lot, but…."

Evelyn grinned. "Kevin is super hot, isn't he?"

"He's your nephew!"

"And I'm not blind." She smirked. "You know I'm right."

Willy huffed and shook his head. "What you are is incorrigible, and you know it." He finished his coffee and checked the time. He still had half an hour before his next class. Willy thought about going to his office, but he didn't want to blow Evelyn off. He just wished she would change the subject.

"Sure I am. But I also have eyes, and Kevin is very easy to look at. I know you noticed," she teased.

It was time to put this conversation to a stop. "Let's talk about something else, okay? I like Kevin, and I think he and I are becoming friends. But I'm not going to jump into a relationship with anyone, no matter how hot he is. I have two kids to think about, and what I do affects them too." He hit her with a stern look.

"So you did notice he was hot," she said and then broke into laughter, with Willy joining her. "So is there anything you need for your new place?"

"Are you kidding? The kids have two outfits each, and the landlord is helping with a couple of bed frames, and she says she has a few pieces of furniture. But other than that, we have nothing. After class I'm going to the consignment shop in Mechanicsburg and the used furniture store on Bedford to see if they have anything that isn't hideous."

"I thought so. I went through what we got stuck with from my mother-in-law, and she had some nice kitchen things. There's dishes, silverware, glasses, and pans… all that sort of stuff. It's boxed, and I'd dearly love to get it out of my basement."

"Oh gosh…." He swallowed hard. "I'd appreciate all of it. I mean, I don't know where I'm going to sleep, but the kids will have beds and rooms of their own. As long as they're safe and happy, that's what counts." He went on to explain where his new place was. "The plan is to move in tomorrow."

"Then I'll have Dennis load the boxes, and we'll bring them over."

Willy checked the time again. "I need to get ready for class, but I'll see you," he said and took care of his mug before leaving the room. He returned to his office, got his materials together, and went to the classroom to set up for his lecture.

BY THE time his class and the afternoon faculty meeting, which actually accomplished very little, were over, Willy was exhausted. His head ached, and he didn't even have time to work on the data for his latest research project. All he wanted to do was get out of there. After checking the time, he raced to the daycare facility and arrived five minutes before late pickup cutoff. Both kids were ready and waiting. He thanked each of their teachers and got them back to the car.

"Daddy, are you going to marry Kevin?" Grant asked. "The teacher for Blue Turtles is marrying his boyfriend in two weeks, so are you going to marry Kevin?" Sometimes he was way too smart for his own good.

"No. Kevin and I are just friends." Yeah, Kevin was a friend that he happened to have dreams about. Dreams that he was not going to even mention to the kids. Hell, he shouldn't even be thinking about those with the kids in the car. "Did you have a fun day at school?"

"Yes. We learned our ABCs." He then proceeded to sing the song out loud and proud. He did great until he sang "*elephant-o-p*." Willy corrected him gently, all the while trying to stifle his laughter. Grant then proceeded to try to teach it to April, who did her best to follow her brother. It was so funny, and the sound of their joy and happiness filled his heart with hope that they wouldn't be scarred by what had happened. His worst fear was that the fire would affect them emotionally. The kids sang all the way to Kevin's, and then they had to sing for Kevin… and then the dogs.

"What's the plan?" Kevin asked once the kids were at the table with their dinner.

"Well, Ellen said she'd have beds at the unit tomorrow, so I figured we'd go ahead and move over there. I thought about looking for furniture after dinner, but I'm worn out."

"Can you do it in the morning?" Kevin asked.

"I'll have to. All I need is a few basic things. Maybe I can head to Target and find some big throw cushions. The kids can use them to sit on the floor. I also thought about going to pick up a television and stand." It just seemed like there weren't enough hours in the day to do everything. "One of the other profs, who happens to be your aunt, has a bunch of kitchen stuff that she said she'd bring over."

"Okay," Kevin said gently. "I should have known you worked with Aunt Evelyn. I just never made the connection."

"Did you want me to make us dinner?" Willy asked.

Kevin shook his head. "It's all set. Our dinner is in the oven and will be ready in about an hour. Once you get the munchkins fed, I figured you could get them bathed and into bed. Then you and I could have a quiet dinner."

"That sounds amazing." He was so relieved.

"Go on upstairs and get cleaned up. I'll sit with these two and get them to eat and stop feeding the dogs."

Kevin was truly a godsend, and Willy lightly kissed him without thinking about it before going right upstairs. He jumped into the shower and washed quickly without giving things too much thought, because if he did, his attention was certain to turn to Kevin, and he didn't have time to let his mind wander to all the wicked places it would certainly like to go.

He got out of the shower, dried off, and dressed in a pair of sweats and T-shirt before going downstairs to find his kids playing "toss the food to the dogs."

"No," he said firmly. "That is for you to eat. And the two of you are going up for your baths and then to bed in a few minutes. And if you don't eat, you aren't getting a cookie before bed." He definitely knew how to motivate his kids, and both of them returned their attention to eating. Once they were done, Willy took both of them upstairs and got them in the tub and then their jammies. He gave each a cookie before bed and then got them to brush their teeth. Each of them wanted a story, so he read to them while the dogs got comfortable.

Once both were settled, he returned to the kitchen, which smelled amazing. "What's this?"

"I made one of the dishes we like at the fire house. It's a chicken and biscuit dish." Kevin pulled a casserole out of the oven and set it on the top of the stove. The entire room smelled of herbs and chicken, making Willy's belly rumble. He hadn't realized how hungry he was until this moment. Kevin got plates and dished some up for both of them. He also got a bottle of wine from the refrigerator and poured them each a glass before bringing everything to the table. "I really hope you like it."

Willy took a small bite. The flavor was rich, the chicken tender, and the biscuit flaky. "It's so good." He closed his eyes for a second before taking another bite, this time getting a bit of carrot. It was a lot like a chicken pot pie, but with biscuits, and he loved it. "Thank you for doing this. Well, for everything." He sipped the wine. "I don't know what we would have done if you hadn't helped us."

"You would have figured everything out. You're smart, and you are determined to land on your feet. You'd have found a place to stay and an apartment. I just helped make some things you'd have done for yourself happen a little faster."

Willy set down his fork. "Do you always do that? Minimize what you do for others?" He had heard Kevin do it before. "You saved my life in that building—and my kids'. I wouldn't have made it out if it wasn't for you. The ceiling of the hall was on fire and it was going to collapse, and we had no way to go but through that mess to the door. Then you took us in, and then you helped find us all a place to live. You did way more than any other firefighter would have."

Kevin shrugged. "What was I supposed to do? Let you all sleep in a tent in the park? I only did what I thought was right. Besides, those kids of yours, they just get hold of your heart and they don't let go."

For a second Willy was jealous of his kids. Or maybe it was just their way of trusting that everything was going to be all right. He always had to think things over from every angle and chew on it until most of the flavor was gone before he could make a decision. Kevin just seemed to know what to do and did it.

"You seemed to win them over very quickly," Willy said. "They're good kids, and you're kind with them."

"I try to be." He continued eating. "But sometimes I wonder what kind of parent I'd be. Being a firefighter, you assess a situation quickly and act fast. That's how you save lives. There isn't time for deliberation. Seconds and minutes can cost lives. But with kids, it's patience, kindness, and taking your time that mean the most."

"That's true. But most of all, you have to love them and be willing to put them before yourself." Willy leaned over the table. "I think as people, each of us is programmed to be selfish to a degree. With children, they have to come first, and I find that's something easy for me to do. They're first in my heart. And…." He swallowed hard. "I think after losing Mark, I just gave everything I had to the kids." And the romantic portion of his life was over. "They were his and mine, and in a way they are all I have left of him. I know it sounds dumb, but the two of us figured we would be raising them together for the next twenty years, and suddenly he was gone." That was a lot more than he intended to say. "I'm sorry. You made me a nice dinner and I'm getting all maudlin and weird." He dabbed his eyes with the napkin. "It's funny, but I don't even have a picture of him."

"What about on your phone? There have to be some that you could restore." Damn it all—Kevin was supposed to get jealous or something, not be nice about this sort of thing.

"There are some there, but those are the ones we took on the fly. In the living room, hanging on the wall, there was a picture of the four of us that we had taken when April was still a baby. I was holding Grant, and Mark held April. It was one of those picture-perfect moments. But that picture is gone."

"Who took it for you?" Kevin asked. "Professional photographers often keep their negatives or electronic images. We could contact them to see if you could get another print."

"I understand, but it was something that Mark arranged for, and I don't know who the photographer was. He had the pictures taken for my birthday that year, and it was a huge surprise. He told me that he was taking the entire family out to dinner to celebrate my birthday and the fact that I had been offered the tenure-track position at Dickinson. So we all got dressed up, and he took us to the photographer's studio before dinner." Willy refused to let himself cry, even though tears were too damn close to the surface.

"It's okay to miss him," Kevin said softly. "And it's okay to mourn for what you lost. Hell, if you didn't, there would be something wrong with you. The kids will be fine because they will remember what you tell them and share with them. But you not only lost Mark once—in a way, you lost part of him again in the fire because some of the things that reminded you of him were lost."

Willy wiped his eyes. "You know, you aren't supposed to be this understanding."

"Why? I know I'm not going to replace Mark in your life, no matter what happens between us. Not that I'm saying that anything has to happen between the two of us. I just mean that…."

Willy smiled. "I know what you're saying, and I know you're right. But a part of me still feels like letting someone new in my life would be letting Mark go. It's dumb, and things don't work like that. But I think I need a chance to get my head and heart around it all. Can you understand?" He felt better that he had explained why he needed to take things slowly, especially after Kevin had gone to the effort to make what was obviously a special dinner.

"Of course I can." He refilled their wineglasses, and they continued eating, the conversation growing quiet for a few minutes. On TV, that pause might have been depicted as uncomfortable, but Willy didn't feel that way. Sometimes silence was nice. "Would you like a little more?"

"Thanks," Willy said as he ate the last of what Kevin had dished up. He got some more, and Kevin refilled his own plate. Then he went to the refrigerator and retrieved a couple bowls of mixed fruit.

"I thought we could have this for dessert. I know it isn't fancy, but after a full day, I don't want anything heavy."

Willy grinned. "The kids would want a cookie."

"You can have one of those too, if you want," Kevin told him. "But they're in bed, and you and I get a few hours of adult time. We can watch a movie, or television, and it doesn't need to be cartoons or Nickelodeon."

"Oh, thank God. There are times when I swear I can hear Mouse House songs in my sleep." He ate the last of his dinner before slowly savoring the fruit. Once they were done, Willy took the dishes to the sink and carried his wineglass into the living room. He let Kevin choose the movie, and they watched the latest Iron Man installment curled together on the sofa.

It was nice being together without worrying about going any further. After a while, his eyes began to drift shut even as they grew closer to the movie's conclusion.

"Are you that tired?"

Willy popped his eyes open. "I don't know. Sometimes I think my attention span has grown smaller and smaller the longer I'm with the kids. They move from topic to topic so quickly that sometimes it's hard to keep up." He looked up and smiled. "Sometimes some of my students remind me of them. They have the hardest time staying on a topic."

"I think all of us have that problem at one point or another. It's part of why we train so hard. At the times of most stress, when your mind has a tendency to go in a million different directions, you have that drilled-in training and muscle memory to rely on. It takes over, and off you go."

"I suppose. But after a while, there's only so much that a body can take. You know? I think things are just catching up with me. I'm so sorry if I'm being a party pooper." He sat up, leaning against Kevin. "I like this." Kevin had paused the movie, and he started it up again. Willy concentrated on the movie and tried to keep awake, but it grew harder. Finally he gave up, leaned his head against Kevin's shoulder, and closed his eyes.

Kevin's arm slipped around him, drawing him closer, and he got comfortable. The movie continued, but Willy relaxed and slowly fell more deeply asleep.

Chapter 6

Kevin knew the moment Willy fell asleep. He stretched out slightly next to him, his head shifting to his lap, and Kevin sat still, watching him, losing interest in the movie. Thumper curled up next to them on the floor, and he reached down and petted him gently before returning his attention to Willy.

"Do you have any idea how gorgeous you are?" he whispered. Then he sat back, turning his attention to the movie, one hand gently caressing Willy's shoulder.

By the time the movie ended, he was tired as well, but he didn't want to leave or disturb Willy, so he simply turned off the television. Thumper whined and nosed against his leg before heading for the stairs. Even his dog was telling him it was time to go to bed. Slowly, he slipped out from under Willy, who stretched out on the sofa. Kevin covered him with a blanket, and Thumper returned and jumped onto the end of the sofa, making himself comfortable next to Willy's legs. "Okay, you can stay here if you want," he told Thumper. Then he turned out the last light and quietly went upstairs.

He'd thought about carrying Willy up, but he didn't want to disturb him. He had been running on adrenaline for days, and goodness knows the kids would be up soon enough in the morning. The thing was that he really didn't want them to leave. He liked having the house full, and the kids made him smile. But it was Willy who touched his heart. Still, it was stupid to think that Willy and his family should stay here with him after just three or four days. They had to get back to their lives, and Kevin needed to do the same, such as it was. That didn't mean he and Willy wouldn't see each other, and they could go to dinner and stuff….

He sighed, because it wouldn't be the same.

Up to this point, their story had been different: two people thrown together by circumstance. But now it was moving to something more commonplace. Kevin liked the exciting part of the story. He liked a bit of unpredictability and the fact that things were different. He didn't want a relationship story that was the same as everyone else's. There was nothing he could do about it now, though, and he couldn't blame Willy for needing stability and not being ready to jump headfirst into anything.

Kevin cleaned up as quietly as he could, not wanting to wake the kids, before slipping into bed and then listening for any sign of Willy. He heard nothing—the house was completely quiet. Rolling over, he closed his eyes, almost willing himself to go to sleep, but it refused to come, and he lay awake with his treadmill of thoughts.

"Daddy." The sound was almost too soft to hear, but Kevin got up, pulled on his robe, and padded down to Grant's room. The boy sat up in bed, rubbing his eyes.

"Your daddy is asleep. But I'm here. What's wrong?" He sat on the side of the bed.

Grant continued rubbing his eyes. "Is it morning?"

Kevin kept himself from chuckling. "No. It's the middle of the night. Go back to sleep."

"But I don't want to miss it," Grant said, still half asleep.

"Miss what?" Kevin asked.

"Going to our new house."

Kevin gently helped him lie back down. "I promise that your daddy and I aren't going to let you sleep through it. Now go back to sleep, and Elsa will make sure everything is okay."

Grant nodded and rolled over. "Kevin, is Elsa going to come live with us? I want her to be my dog."

Kevin probably should have seen this coming. The kids had bonded with the dogs. "This is their home, and Elsa would miss Benjamin and Thumper and me. But you can come over and visit Elsa a lot if you like. I promise. Okay?" He hoped he had said the right thing.

"Okay. I come visit her every day." He seemed happy, and Kevin sat with him for a few minutes before quietly leaving the room. He partially closed the door and went back to bed, proud of himself for how he'd handled things with Grant. He was going to miss them all, but it wasn't like he would never see them again. At least that was what he hoped. Things would just be different.

Kevin rolled over and tried to sleep once more, eventually slipping into a restless slumber.

"WHY HAVE you been such a grump bucket today?" Chase asked as he closed the plans for the apartment complex in frustration.

"Because there is nothing here that explains why the fire spread so damned fast. Even without the working sprinklers, it shouldn't have done that. As far as I can tell, the building was up to code."

"Maybe there's something in the codes that should be examined," Chase offered with a sigh before hitting him with a steely gaze. "But there's more than that going on."

"Willy and the kids are moving into their own place today. They were packing their things and heading over to spend the day getting the place ready." Kevin didn't like the way that made him feel, though he knew he had no right to be this way. Chase and the guys didn't deserve to be around him when he was all grumpy and shit.

"That's a good thing. They're rebuilding their lives." He rolled his eyes. "I know you like the guy, and that's cool, but this doesn't mean any of that has to change. He'll have a place of his own like a normal person, and those kids need a stable place to call their home again." Kevin wanted to argue with Chase, but of course he was right and Kevin was just being unreasonable. "When are you off shift?"

Kevin checked the time on his phone. "Half an hour. The chief let me go a few hours early in case I needed to help Willy. I'm on call, though."

"Then let's get out of here. There are questions about this building that these plans are never going to answer. But maybe if we can talk to Willy, he can answer some of them. After all, he lived there, and he's a smart guy. Let's see if somehow he can provide some of the answers that we need."

"Okay." Kevin was more than ready to get out of here. He had been on edge all day for no good reason, so maybe seeing Willy and the kids would help. Kevin told the chief where they were going, and they headed out to Willy's new place, which was quiet. After parking, he knocked on the door, and Willy answered it with April and Grant right behind him.

"Kevin!" Grant raced over and practically leapt into his arms. "Come see my new room." He dragged Kevin into a small bedroom with a bed and a few toys. "Daddy says that this is all mine and I don't have to share with the baby anymore." He bounced, he was so excited. "I even have my own big-boy bed." It was sparse, but the bed was made, and it looked homey.

"He's so excited," Willy said from the doorway.

"Are you all moved in?" Kevin asked.

"Yeah. Your aunt brought over a bunch of kitchen things that I'm just going through." He held out his hand, and Grant took it, letting Willy take him back to the living room, where he plopped down on one of the floor pillows to watch TV in the otherwise empty room. "I found a sofa today and a chair. The sofa is a floral pattern, but I ordered a slipcover, so that will help. I also found a table and chairs on Nextdoor, but I need to pick those up."

"You can borrow the truck," Kevin offered. Chase cleared his throat when Kevin left him in the doorway. "Do you have a minute? Chase and I have some questions."

"Sure," Willy said.

"It's about your other place," he added softly, and Willy nodded. "Can we go to the kitchen?" He didn't want the kids to hear them talking in case they got upset.

Willy led them into the other room, which had a number of boxes sitting on the counter with Kevin's aunt's distinctive handwriting on the outside. "Can you tell us what it was like living there?"

"Well, a shoebox. The walls were kind of thin, like I told Kevin. I always had to watch TV very quietly or it would wake the kids. And there were a lot of times when I could hear the neighbors. It was like there was nothing at all between the units. I always thought there should have been some sort of fire break or something to dampen sound, but there was nothing there."

Chase made notes. "The plans show insulation between the units."

"There couldn't have been much, and we could sometimes hear the people below us. I had rugs down in every room of the house because I didn't want the downstairs neighbors to hear the kids."

Kevin nodded. "What about the smoke alarms? We know they didn't go off, and neither did the sprinklers."

"Yeah. Have you looked into the other buildings?" Willy asked.

"Yes. The fire marshals and the building inspectors have been through them with a fine-toothed comb. Everything worked the first time. It's like this building, the one you lived in, was completely forgotten."

"But it wasn't. The management was around, and they maintained the building. I saw them in and out. Last Thanksgiving, my oven didn't work. They had someone there to replace it, on Thanksgiving, within an hour, and they took a hundred dollars off the rent the next month for the inconvenience. They were good people."

"But things didn't work," Kevin said.

"Maybe they didn't know they didn't work, or they thought they did," Willy said. "Why would you test all of the other buildings and not ours? I mean, with the sprinkler system, you can only test it so far. You can't have it go off and wet everything down. So what if that worked, but the rest didn't? I don't know. But it seems like there's a mystery here." Willy leaned against the counter. "Who built the building?"

Chase pulled out his notes. "Wilson and Marshall built the complex."

Willy pushed away as he shook his head. "No, who actually built the building? Is there a difference?"

Kevin gaped, wishing he had thought of that. "Maybe it was a different contractor." He pulled out his phone and called the codes office. They had to keep records of all permits and inspections. He requested the information he needed and then hung up. "They're going to call me back."

Willy shrugged. "If the other buildings are different from this one, then why is that true? What's the cause? A contractor isn't going to build three buildings and then cheat on everything on the fourth. It makes no sense. After doing three, they'd do the fourth the exact same way as the others. Then everything would simply be easier. Repetition makes it more efficient, so why do something different?"

"Maybe because it was the last unit and they decided to cut corners?" Kevin supplied as his phone rang. He answered it.

"The whole complex was built by the same development company, but the contractor for the first three units had financial problems, and the last unit was built by Kraft and Hobson out of Philadelphia. They are still in business, mostly in the Philadelphia area."

"Perfect," Kevin told her. "Thanks. That helps us a lot." He ended the call and relayed the information. "So it sounds like we have our answer. But what do we do with it?"

Chase smiled. "I'm going to include it in the fire report and forward it to the police. The various insurance companies are going to be interested in that information as well. They are going to have to pay out claims, so they might try to go after them."

"True. But there has to be evidence that we can provide," Kevin said.

"Okay, but be damned careful. I went by what's left of the place, and it's kind of frightening. The walls look about ready to cave in at any time." Willy looked worried at the idea of them visiting what was left of his old building.

"We always are. Right now, it isn't safe for anyone to enter. We're waiting until the borough has someone look at it before we go in. But eventually we're going to have to. If there was something wrong with how it was constructed, then we're going to need to make sure that none of the other buildings these people worked on are like this. That could involve law enforcement and even the state."

Willy nodded slowly, but it was clear he wasn't a fan of the idea.

"Is there anything we can do to help you?" Chase asked.

"Not really. I have to go through the kitchen things that I have, but other than that there isn't much to do. I mean, I guess we'll get the things we need over time. It's all I can do until the insurance comes through, and even then, I don't want to go out and buy a whole bunch of new stuff just because I can."

"I get that."

April stood on her pillow, then jumped up and down before plopping back down once more.

"There's a lot I just don't seem to know right now, and things for the kids come first. I need to get them toys and books and things."

Kevin stepped closer to him. "I don't go into the station until noon on Saturday. If you want, we could hit the yard sales this weekend. People are always selling kids' stuff. We might be able to find some books, toys, and even clothes for them."

Willy smiled up at him like the sun had just come out. "Sure. We can do that. It sounds like fun, and you never know what we may find."

And on top of that, Kevin and Willy would get to spend some time together.

Kevin and Chase stayed a little while longer before heading back to the station. "That wasn't very helpful."

"Yes, it was," Kevin countered. "This was the second time that Willy told me about how he lived in that apartment. Do you remember how the plans showed that the walls between units were solid and that they acted as firebreaks? Those were missing. In this unit, the walls were just timber and sheetrock with whatever basic loadbearing walls that were needed. I went into one of the other units, and the walls in the central halls were block making up a stable central column. Those walls also acted as breaks to keep fire from jumping all around the building. There were no such features in the one that burned."

"So you're saying that you believe that the new contractor… what? Altered the plans they were using and did their best to cover it up? What about the inspectors?" Chase asked.

"I don't know. Maybe they gave them the plans they were using. But this building is different." Kevin made a turn and drove Chase to the scene of the fire. "Don't go inside, but take a look." He waited while Chase hurried over to the barrier and peered through one of the window openings.

"There's nothing there at all. Just a large open space."

"Yeah. Now let's go over there," he said, leading Chase to the other building. As one of the residents was leaving, he explained why they were there and went into the vestibule. "Look there. That is block, and so is that, and according to the plans we saw, those walls bisect the entire building and go all the way up. So a fire isn't going to skip from one side to the other. The floors here are also solid wood, so the fire is going to have to burn through the ceilings and insulation, and then the floor above before going upward. That takes time. And the other building burned way too fast. So I'd say that corners were severely cut, not only in the walls, but in the fire-suppression systems, and, I'm willing to bet, anything else they possibly could."

"But how did they get that past the inspectors? Do you think they paid them off?"

"God, no. I think they overwhelmed the inspectors with misdirection. They'd fix one problem and create two more. The inspectors would catch some of them, but by the time the building was finished, it was a piece of shit put together with shell games and faked tests. The construction team got paid, moved on, and the owners took possession of a ticking time bomb that went off five days ago." He shook his head. "Now that we suspect what happened, we need to gather as much evidence as we possibly can and speak to the inspector who worked on this project, if they're still with the borough, which I'm betting is unlikely."

"True." They returned to the truck, and Kevin drove them back to the station just in time to join the team on a fire call. Paperwork was going to have to wait.

Chapter 7

The kids were up, dressed, and ready by the time Kevin arrived on Saturday morning. "Where are the dogs?" Grant asked as soon as Kevin came through the door.

"How about I bring them for a visit next time, okay?" He smiled, and Grant seemed happy.

"You got the furniture?"

Willy smiled. "I was able to pay a few of my students to help me out. They needed the extra money, and I got the use of their muscles for a few hours." The sofa was in great shape, and with the navy slipcover, it worked with the other things he'd found, including a rug and a couple of side tables and lamps. He had also found a bed and had a new mattress delivered, so at least he had the very basic things. The one item he was still looking for was a kitchen table and chairs, but he hoped he could find those soon.

"Get toys?" April asked.

"Let's go see what we can find." Kevin lifted her into his arms. "Maybe we can find something you like."

"I want a stuffed lion and a whale and a sheep."

"Then let's see what we can find." They all piled into Willy's car. "I checked out a few ads, and there are three sales on the south side of town. We could go there before heading to the north side. I made a list of addresses." Kevin gave him the first one, and Willy drove over and parked just up the block.

As soon as he got her out, April ran down the sidewalk like she was going to get there as fast as she could to see if there was anything she wanted. Grant went after her with Kevin close behind. By the time he arrived, April stood next to a dollhouse with huge eyes. It had a ton of furniture and a few dolls. Grant stood off to the side because it seemed there were only girl toys.

"Maybe the next one will have something for you," Kevin soothed as Grant crossed his arms over his chest. There were times when Grant reminded him so much of himself.

"How much is the dollhouse?" Willy asked as April vibrated with excitement.

The lady came down from the porch. "I'm asking forty dollars for it. It has all the furniture, and if you plug it in, the lights work." She forced a smile.

"Will you take thirty?" Willy asked, and she thought about it. They arrived at thirty-five, and Willy bought it. Kevin maneuvered it into the center of the back seat between the car seats, and they raced home, where Kevin got the dollhouse inside before they returned to the next sale. It was a total bust, but the third one held gold. Grant found three trucks, April got a stuffed hippo, and Willy found some books to read to the kids. It was a great stop.

"Daddy, I'm hungry," April said as she hugged the hippo in her car seat, once everything had been loaded and they were on their way.

"Me too," Grant chimed in.

"I fed both of them, I swear," Willy told Kevin softly as he navigated to the next address Kevin gave him. Once they arrived, he opened the glove box and pulled out a bag of Cheerios, which he handed to April. "Can you share some with Grant?" She gave him her unhappy face, but as soon as his back was turned, she offered some to her brother.

"I don't see much here," Kevin said. "Let me check it out, and if there's nothing, we can head on." He got out, and Willy made sure the kids were okay. They munched on the cereal and seemed happy enough. Turning his attention to Kevin, he watched as he looked things over. As he returned to the car, he answered his phone and hung up again after a brief conversation, then jumped back in.

"What's up? Do you need me to take you to the station?"

"No. It's okay," he said just above a whisper, after glancing back at the kids, who were engrossed in their treat. "That was Chase. He told me that they were called back to your old building. Someone set what was left of it on fire. This time it was arson. He said the entire place smelled of petroleum when they arrived, with thick black smoke rising up. What was left went up fast and collapsed." He banged his hand against the dashboard. "I had hoped to be able to get in there to see what we could find about how the place had been built and maybe some clues to the fire-suppression systems, but that's gone, along with everything else. According to Chase, there is nothing left of the structure at all. We'll be sifting through ash and debris to find anything." He sighed loudly.

"I'm sorry. I wish there was something more I could do to help."

Kevin grew quiet as Willy made his way to the next sale. This looked more promising, so he got the kids out, and they looked around while Kevin made more phone calls.

"Daddy!" A happy cry went up as April hurried across the yard to a plastic grocery cart filled with plastic food and other items. She immediately began wheeling it around the yard.

"My daughter played with that for hours sometimes," the lady said. "But she outgrew it."

Willy's own daughter was halfway across the yard. "April, please come back." He hadn't even had a chance to check the price.

"She can have it for five if it makes her that happy," the lady said, and Willy nodded.

"We lost everything when our apartment building burned, and I'm trying…." He hadn't meant to say anything, and the words got caught in his throat. He thought they had been moving on, but it still sucked that everything they had was gone. Dammit, April shouldn't have to be so excited over an old play grocery cart. "And thank you. I'll take the cart."

Kevin got out of the car and joined him, his expression confused and maybe a touch angry. He came right over and slipped his arm around Willy's waist. "Grant, did you find something?"

He sat on the ground looking in a box, his eyes wide. "I was coming out here and found that on my way," the lady said. "This was my mother's home, and she had a ton of things for the kids. She was always buying things she thought they might like and then putting them away… and forgetting about them. That was in the front closet, probably for my sister's boys. Who knows."

Grant raced over and took Willy by the hand, too excited for words. "Legos," he said, and Willy looked inside the box. There were a couple of building sets and a bunch of loose building blocks.

"I was going to put twenty on that, but take it for ten," the woman said as other people pulled up. Willy got his money out for what both kids wanted, and Kevin carried their treasures back and placed them in the trunk.

"Can we eat now?" Grant asked as soon as the car doors were closed.

"Yes. We can get something to eat," Willy said. "What do you want?"

"Chickens," Grant declared. "Wendy chicken with sauce."

April was quiet, and Willy figured she would be happy with a few french fries, so they drove to Wendy's and got a small order of chicken nuggets and a small french fry. Kevin ordered what he wanted while Willy got the kids settled in a booth.

"I got you something too. I know you take care of the kids and forget about yourself." He placed a full order of nuggets in front of Willy and offered some of his fries.

"Thanks." He hadn't even realized he was hungry until he took the first bite. The kids were busy eating, so Willy felt like he could relax a little. "Is everything all right?"

"No. I keep going over things and coming up empty. Why would someone set fire to a burned-out shell?"

"Because they thought there must be something for someone to find. I know that the building is gone, but I had a few friends there. I could call them so you and Chase could talk to them as well about what it was like to live there. I'd also talk to the maintenance guys for the complex. They had to deal with the building in a way no one else did. They might be able to help you. It's not like they built the place or anything, but they did have to deal with whatever messes the people who built the place left behind."

"The police would have spoken with them already, I'm sure."

"True, but they would question them like police. Did they see anything and stuff like that. If you talked to them, you would ask questions like a fireman. A big difference, I think."

Kevin leaned over the table and kissed him. "You're a genius, you know that?"

"Ewww," came the chorus from next to them.

"Daddy and Kevin, sitting in a tree, k-i-s-s-i-n-g," Grant sang. There were times when Willy hated preschool.

"That's enough. Your daddy was being brilliant," Willy said. "Now finish eating. You were so hungry." He fake glowered at them, and they giggled and each picked up a fry.

Kevin made a call, probably to Chase, and they talked briefly.

"He's going to set up a meeting with them for early next week."

"Good. I keep wondering if there really is something so bad that someone would set fire to what was left. I mean, really, I wonder if they realize that by doing this they're drawing attention to themselves…." He chewed on a nugget but barely tasted it.

"What are you thinking?" Kevin asked.

"Well, there was a fire and the building burned down. Plenty of questions have arisen, and people want answers. That's reasonable. So burn down what's left and make getting them even harder while at the same time convincing everyone that there's something to find?"

Kevin nodded. "That's a theory."

"Yeah, sure. But we already knew there was something there to find."

"Proof that construction was faulty," Kevin supplied, but Willy shook his head. "You don't think so?"

"Oh, I do, but what if it's more than that? What if by setting fire to what was already damaged…." He sighed. "Okay, this is going to sound nuts. But I suspect that with the one building having burned, the others would be inspected and reviewed for safety reasons. But with the second fire, every eye is back on the old building. So what if the purpose of that was to pull attention away from the other buildings? What if there is a bigger issue that someone is trying to keep secret?"

Kevin groaned. "You sound like one of those wild conspiracy theorists on television. And yet you may have a point. Chase and I looked at the plans for all the buildings, but we concentrated on the ones for the one that burned. I mean, that was where the issue was. But the chief was already talking about inspections and a review of the other structures to make sure they weren't in a similar state and were safe for the residents there."

"Of course. And you need to make sure that is still completed. Because there is something going on. No one torches an already burned building unless they are really afraid and have something pretty big to hide. Why risk it?" The whole thing seemed stupid, and yet it had happened, which in his mind meant there had to be a reason for it. "Unless there is something else they're trying to hide."

"If there's something there, we'll figure it out." Kevin finished eating his snack and then threw away all the trash once they were done. "There are a few more sales that we can look at. It's getting late—a lot of them end at noon—but maybe we can drive by a few to see if there is anything left."

"Okay." Willy got the kids belted into their car seats and slipped into the driver's seat. It was a warm day, so he lowered all the windows as they tooled through town.

"Daddy, can we play Legos when we get home?" Grant asked.

"Yes, of course. I think I have—" he began and cut himself off before turning. "I was going to say that I thought I might have my old Legos in a box in my closet, but if I did, they'd be gone now. It's so strange to think that everything from before is just… not there anymore."

Kevin nodded. "Do your parents have anything?"

"No. Everything was turned over to me when I moved out years ago. When Mom and Dad moved to Arizona, they took only what they needed. Mom was never one for clutter, and I guess she went through everything in their downsizing efforts." Still, it would have been nice to have had some of the things from when he was a kid to pass on to April and Grant. But that wasn't to be.

"Do your parents know about the fire?"

"Oh, yes. I told them about it the other day. They asked if I wanted them to come, but I said we were doing okay and that they should come for a visit for Thanksgiving like they had originally planned. They only have so much money, and if things are in an uproar, then my mother goes into work mode because she can't stand any sort of flux. Their moving to Arizona was planned in detail, and Mom would drive me crazy trying to manage everything now." He pulled to a stop at the light at the square. "I think Mom will like the new place more than she did the old one. There's more space, for one thing, and I can't wait to tell her that Ellen said it was okay to put in a play structure in the back. Mom will no doubt pick one out and have it delivered and installed." There was nothing wrong with that as far as he was concerned.

The light changed and they continued north, out into the ABC streets. "The next one is on D Street."

Willy made the turn and drove slowly past what was left. It looked like someone had been cleaning out their kitchen. They continued to the next one, and Willy drove past this one with no interest. But down the block was another, and he pulled right off.

"A table and chairs," Kevin said. "I'll stay with the kids. You check it out. If it works, I can get the truck to pick it up."

"Okay. Let me see what it looks like." He left the engine running and got out of the car. The homeowners looked like they were packing up. "Are the table and chairs still for sale?" he asked.

An older man used a cane to make his way over. "Yup. I wanted fifty for the set. It's been in the garage for years, and I just want to get rid of it. Nobody even looked at it, but for twenty bucks and the fact that I don't have to haul it back, you can have it."

Willy looked it over. The chairs and table were solid wood, probably maple, with a medium brown finish. The table was round, with a leaf and six chairs. "Sounds good. We need to get the truck to pick it up, but we'll be back in twenty minutes." He paid for it.

"I'll leave it right where it is for you." The man pocketed the money and put a Sold sign on the set. "You saved my legs and back."

"And it was just what I needed." Willy returned to the car. "It's perfect. I bought it, and we need to pick it up right away."

"Then drop me at the house and I'll come get it," Kevin offered.

Willy drove down West Street toward his new home. He parked out front, and Kevin hopped in the truck and took off. Willy got the kids inside and unloaded everything. The kids immediately began playing with their new toys. Willy kept the Legos in the trunk until Kevin returned because he didn't want Grant tearing apart the building sets.

Fortunately his son was more than happy to play with his trucks, running them around the living room floor while his sister did the same thing with her shopping cart. By the time he put the books away and returned, April was sitting on the floor crying.

"What's going on?"

"She has to find the food," Grant explained as April continued crying over her empty cart.

"Come on, let's find the food together." He could see where most of it was, so he helped her get the cart, and once she got the hang of the game, she seemed to enjoy finding the plastic food and putting it in the cart. Once they had it all, she pushed the cart away to keep it from Grant. Willy sat on the sofa with a cup of coffee and took a moment to give himself a rest.

"Grant!" April yelled.

"Leave her food alone," Willy commanded, and Grant pouted as he returned to his trucks. Sometimes they were predictable. Thankfully they were too young to be truly devious, but he knew that phase was coming—along with the gray hair that went with it.

Kevin came through the front door. "I got the table." He hefted it alone and set it in the kitchen; then they brought in the chairs and the leaf together. "It's really nice."

"Legos?" Grant asked before either of them could sit down.

"I'll go get them," Willy said and went out to retrieve the box from the back of the car. He opened the trunk and lifted it out, then closed the trunk. He nearly dropped it when a man strode across the street, his expression intent. "Can I help you?"

The man approached boldly. "You need to quit opening your mouth. Keep it closed and you and your kids will be fine. But keep running it and you'll wish you'd clammed up." He tried to take the Lego box, and Willy kicked out. The man's eyes grew wide, and then they watered before he grabbed himself and fell to the sidewalk. Willy left him and went inside, closed the door, and locked it.

"What was that about?" Kevin asked as he took the box and placed it on the table.

"Some guy. I think he was threatening me. Then he grabbed for the box, so I got him in the family jewels. I think he might be gone now."

"What did he say?"

"Something about talking too much. He sounded like he got his lines from a bad gangster movie. He isn't going to come back here. If he does, well, he'll be walking really funny. I'm not afraid of some...." He stopped himself from swearing, but only just. "Anyway, we've got Legos." He took the building sets out of the box, and Grant climbed onto one of the chairs before tipping the box over and spilling all the remaining loose Legos onto the table and floor.

"Buddy," Kevin said, "now you have to pick up all the ones on the floor."

Grant looked at Kevin like he was crazy.

"Grant, please pick them up."

"But Daddy, I want to play." He began putting pieces together, and Willy groaned.

"Fine, but you'll still have to get them all off the floor." He was trying to teach Grant to pick up after himself, and for the most part he'd been about as successful as getting a tornado to avoid trailer parks. Grant didn't even look up from the Legos, instantly enthralled in whatever he was building.

Kevin, on the other hand, checked out the sets. "These were in the box?"

"Yeah. I didn't pay much attention to them. I figured they could be used for blocks if they weren't anything interesting. Why?"

"They were never opened." He pulled out his phone as Willy peered over his shoulder. "This Mustang model has been out of distribution for years, and so has this one. These are pretty rare, judging by how much people paid for them online. I'd put these aside for now and let him play all he wants with the blocks."

"Cool." Grant didn't seem interested, and if he were to open them, he would probably only add them to the block pile anyway.

"You play too?" Grant asked Kevin. Thankfully, he scooped up some of the blocks from the floor before sitting down.

"Grant, Kevin has to go to work in a few minutes," Willy cautioned, and got a pout in response.

"No. He stay and play," Grant said as though he had the last word. "Work is yucky. Legos are fun."

Willy shared a chuckle with Kevin. "I know. Grant is going to grow up to be the autocratic ruler of a small country. Grantsylvania." He rolled his eyes as Kevin handed Grant what looked like a blue frog. Grant smiled and set it aside. "What are you making?"

"Elephant," he proclaimed and added more blocks to a multicolored lump.

"I really do have to go," Kevin said.

Willy walked him to the front door. "Thank you. We had a great time and…." He felt at a loss for words, but he hugged Kevin and inhaled his clean, rich scent. Then he backed away slightly before placing his hands on either side of his face, looking into his eyes. "It was a really nice morning. Maybe you can come back after your shift."

"I work until almost eleven."

Willy nodded. "The kids should be in bed, and it will be just the two of us if we're lucky."

Kevin's eyes darkened, and he slipped his hands around Willy before letting them slide down so they cupped his butt. Willy groaned softly, desire sweeping through him.

"I know you probably have things you need to do…."

"I'd love to. Maybe I could bring the dogs. They will have been alone all day, and…."

"Sure. The kids will love that, I'm sure." Kevin was warm, strong, and it felt so good to be held for a while. "I know you have to go—"

Kevin took possession of his lips, cutting off whatever Willy was going to say, not that he could remember a word. Then Kevin pulled away and opened the door. "I'll see you tonight." He kissed Willy again quickly before hurrying off. Willy's gaze followed him to his truck, and once Kevin was gone, he checked the area around the house to make sure no one was hanging around and then closed the door and locked it.

"Daddy, my elephant broke," Grant yelled.

Then April hurried in, teary-eyed. "I lost food." It looked like it was going to be one of those days.

Chapter 8

KEVIN STANK of fire, sweat, and God knows what else. One call after another for the entire shift had him nearly completely worn out. Fortunately his relief was on time, and he grabbed his gear bag and got out the damned door before something else happened and he ended up staying the entire night. He tossed his bag into the back of the truck and drove home.

When he opened the door, the dogs all crowded around for attention. He gave them pets and treats and let them out to pee before hurrying upstairs, where he showered quickly and pulled on a T-shirt and light sweatpants. "Come on, guys. You want to see the kids?" he called after putting some of their food and treats in a bag, and they all hurried to the front door. Kevin locked up and left with his little pack. He opened the truck door, and all three jumped inside, excited to get to ride. "You need to be quiet when we go inside." He spoke to the dogs like they were people, but they'd do what they did anyway.

The ride took less than five minutes, and Willy must have been watching, because he opened the door as they pulled up. Kevin let the dogs out, and they trooped right past Willy into the house. "I take it they were excited."

Kevin closed the truck door and locked it before Willy wound his arms around his neck. "I've been waiting for you."

"I guess so. How were the kids today?"

"Wound up tight as drums. They played with their new toys all day. I swear I'm going to find plastic food in April's bed, and Grant wanted to sleep with his Lego elephant. But in one victory, I did get him to pick up what was on the floor."

"How?"

"He wanted a cookie," Willy said. "Okay, I bribed him, but it worked." He rested his head on Kevin's shoulder right there on the sidewalk.

"Let's go inside." The things Kevin wanted, he did not want the damned neighbors to see. Willy just held him, so Kevin slowly moved both of them inside. Once he closed the door and locked up, Willy practically climbed him like a tree. Kevin lifted Willy into his arms, and Willy wrapped his legs around Kevin's waist. "I take it you've been thinking about me."

"Damn right," Willy muttered.

"Are you sure? You were the one who wanted to take things slow."

Willy growled. "We did that. Slow sucks, and not in a good way." He kissed Kevin hard, stealing his breath. Kevin tightened his hold on Willy, one hand around his back while the other supported his amazing ass. Damn, he wanted all of this—now.

"Daddy, I'm firsty."

Willy stilled and then put his head on Kevin's shoulder for a second. Then he unwound himself and stepped away. He turned and went over to Grant and took him by the hand.

"Let's get you a drink, and then you can go back to bed."

"Can I sleep wif you?" Grant asked. Kevin could feel his night of passion slipping away.

"No. But Kevin brought the dogs with him, so I bet Elsa will be in to keep you company." Willy ran the water and got Grant's drink before putting him back into bed. Elsa followed them and disappeared into Grant's room.

Kevin sat on the sofa, and Willy left Grant's room before checking on April. Then he returned to the living room and flopped down on the sofa, with Thumper joining them for some attention of his own. "Each kid has their protector, and if I get one more request for a drink of water or a cookie, I think my head is going to explode."

"We can't have that," Kevin said softly. "No heads exploding. It's yucky and a real mess to clean up." He grinned, hoping making light of it would get Willy to smile. And thankfully it did. "The kids are in bed and the house is quiet." He ran his fingers through Willy's hair, and he closed his eyes, breathing deeply, angling his face upward. "And you are stunning."

Willy snickered and reddened. "I am not. I'm just a skinny professor of economics. You're the one who's stunning, with all your hunkiness." He pulled away. "I can't figure out what the hell you see in me. You could have any guy you wanted just by crooking your finger at them, and you wouldn't need to put up with kids and God knows what else."

Kevin humphed and then stood and hoisted Willy over his shoulder.

"What are you doing?" he whispered intently and then squeaked as Kevin carried him through the house.

"Sometimes you talk too much." Kevin carried him to the back bedroom and kicked the door closed. Then he set Willy down on the bed with a bounce.

"But what I said is true." That lower lip stuck out the same way Grant's did when he made one of his pronouncements. Like father, like son.

Kevin stood over the bed. "Bullshit," he said and leaned over. He held Willy's gaze, daring him to contradict him as he glared. "You see yourself one way, but that doesn't mean that I do or anyone else does." He pulled off his shirt, and Willy's eyes widened. "I know you like my muscles. I saw that the one night when you were staying with me." He tugged at Willy's shirt, pulling it over his head. "And you're sleek and sexy, and you don't get to contradict me. Understand?" He kissed Willy in case he argued, then pressed him into the mattress as he climbed onto the bed. "I want you, and I have for a while."

"But I don't understand why."

Kevin smiled. "Then let me show you." He took both of Willy's hands and pushed them upward. Then he held them there, kissing him hard, taking possession of those sweet lips. Once he had Willy gasping, he nuzzled his neck and down to his chest, where he sucked at a pert nipple until Willy writhed. Now that was sexy. The way Willy responded to him was the sexiest thing Kevin had ever seen. Looks were one thing, but this was something else entirely.

"Kevin," Willy whimpered as he squirmed.

"You stay right where you are," he growled softly, sucking harder as Willy arched his back. He was getting desperate for more, Kevin could feel it, and that was amazing. He was determined to take his time, but the way Willy wriggled his hips and squirmed under him nearly became his undoing. There was nothing on earth more attractive than someone whose body seemed automatically connected with yours.

"But that means I can't touch you," Willy said.

Kevin drew close enough that Willy's scent surrounded him. "You'll get your chance for that. But for right now, you just have to let me take the lead." He wondered about how things had been between Willy and Mark, but he didn't want to ask at a moment like this. Instead, he took in all of Willy's curves, the way his belly fluttered when Kevin ran his hands over his smooth skin, and the way his hips stuck out just a little. He nuzzled at the skin above the line of the waistband of Willy's sweats before tugging them downward. Willy's breath hitched, and Kevin inhaled deeply, taking in Willy's musky scent, letting it grow more intense as he pressed the fabric lower.

"You know this isn't fair," Willy said.

"That may be true, but I think this is perfection." He pushed the light sweats lower and down off his hips until Willy's cock bounded out and stretched up toward his belly button. No matter how Willy might tease, he was definitely turned on, and Kevin ran his lips up the length before slipping the head between them and sucking Willy deep.

The sounds that filled the room were even hotter than Willy tasted. Slowly he sank lower, taking all of Willy into his mouth, before running his tongue along the lower ridge of his cock.

"Jesus, are you really trying to kill me?" Willy asked as he thrust his hips forward. Kevin stilled him and backed away before taking all of him once more.

Somehow Willy managed to get his sweats off his legs and onto the floor, which gave Kevin greater access. And he was all about the access. When he ran a hand up Willy's leg, those long, beautiful legs parted, and he teased Willy's balls before pressing a finger to his opening.

"Kevin!" Willy cried and shivered under him.

"Do you want me to stop?" he asked. "I can just back away if that's what you want."

Willy wound his arms around Kevin's neck and pulled him close. "Don't you fucking dare."

"Good." Kevin pressed a finger in up to the first knuckle, and Willy groaned and damn near came unglued. Kevin smiled before sucking him again, this time doing his best to give Willy everything he wanted.

Willy's breathing became ragged, and he held on tightly while Kevin played him like an instrument. He wanted Willy to know just how he felt about him. It was important for Willy to know that Kevin saw him for who he was. Whatever Willy's experience had been before, Kevin intended to make him feel like the center of the universe, and if that meant putting him first and delaying his own gratification, then so be it. Sex was meant to be fun, but it was also something that required generosity and patience, at least in his opinion, and from Willy's reaction, both seemed to have been lacking for him… and were just what Willy needed.

Kevin sank his finger into Willy, loving how he shook on the bed. "I'm so ready."

Kevin pulled back. "What do you want?"

Willy lifted his head from the mattress, his eyes blazing. "I want you to make love to me."

Those were the words he had been waiting for. Kevin let his finger slip from inside Willy's heat and moved away from the bed. He toed off his shoes and stripped away the last of his clothing, letting Willy see the man he truly was.

"Damn," Willy sighed.

"Looks are just that. It's the person on the inside that counts." He stalked back to the bed. "I've had physical jobs of one sort or another for most of my life. In the winter I go to the gym to stay fit so I don't pile on the weight, but otherwise, my work keeps me fit."

"Mine just gives me chair butt." He sat up, and Kevin drew closer, sliding between Willy's legs, kissing him as he pressed him against the pillows. "I still don't understand what you see in me. I'm a father of two who's exhausted and trying to rebuild his life."

"Where did this lack of self-worth come from? You're, what, twenty-eight, have a doctorate, and you're on your way to a full professorship. You have come up with ideas that no one else ever thought of. Now that's sexy. So don't put yourself down. Not everyone can have muscles like me." He flexed his arms. "Just like not everyone can have a mind like yours. So be happy with the gifts you've been given."

Willy kissed him. "And I suppose we need to be happy when we find someone who appreciates those gifts." He ran his hands over Kevin's arms and then down his chest. "Because I like these particular gifts… a lot." Kevin chuckled as Willy tugged him closer. "Why don't you show me just how amazing those gifts of yours can be."

Kevin grinned. "Oh, you want to see?"

"And feel."

Kevin pressed Willy to the mattress, letting his weight settle on him. He hoped he wasn't too heavy, but Willy held him right back, the kisses building quickly to the point that Kevin could barely think straight. Not that it mattered, because at this particular moment, thinking was vastly overrated.

Heat built between them as each explored the other. It was like unwrapping a gift and finding something inside that you never knew you wanted, but as soon as you had it, you wondered how you ever got along without it. That was what this moment felt like to Kevin. "Do you have supplies?" Kevin should have brought some with him, but he had nothing. And as soon as he asked the question, he knew the answer. There had been way too many things going on for that sort of preparation. But it didn't matter, because there were many ways to make love to someone else.

KEVIN LAY in the bed as Willy rolled over next to him, sliding a hand over his chest. Willy snuffled lightly and then seemed to settle. Thumper pushed the door open and quietly came into the room. Kevin smiled, and Thumper jumped up and made himself comfortable at the foot of the bed.

"What's that?" Willy asked.

"Shhh. Just Thumper joining us," Kevin explained, and Willy hummed and got out of the bed, his bare butt bouncing as he went into the bathroom. Kevin waited for him to return and climb back into the bed.

"When do you have to go to work tomorrow?"

"I work from two till eleven or so." He tugged Willy to him. "Just go back to sleep. The kids will be awake soon enough."

Willy chuckled. "Tell me about it. I keep hoping the kids will learn to sleep later, but as soon as the sun lightens up their rooms, they're awake and ready to go. I tried heavy curtains at the apartment, and it did nothing. They seemed to know when the sun was up." He yawned and drew closer.

"Don't worry about it. Just let yourself sleep. I'll be here, and the kids each have a dog to keep watch over them. And who knows, the dogs might encourage them to sleep in." After all, anything was possible.

"We'll see." Willy seemed to settle, and soon his breathing evened out. Kevin lay awake for a while, but finally fell asleep.

"DADDY." GRANT came into the room with Elsa following him. She jumped onto the bed, joining Thumper.

"He's still asleep. How about you go to your room and get dressed? I'll come in and we can play Legos or something."

Grant turned to leave, and Kevin pulled on his sweatpants just in time to hear him start heaving. He hurried out and lifted Grant, managing to get him into the bathroom before he threw up. The poor kid was hot, and his hair stuck to his head. Kevin gave him some water once he was done. "Do you feel like you're going to throw up again?"

Grant hesitated and then shook his head. "But my head hurts."

"Okay." He carried Grant to the bedroom and put him in bed with Willy. Then he checked on April, who was still sound asleep. Benjamin lifted his head as soon as he peered in the room and then lowered it again as if to say that she was okay.

He returned to Willy's room, where Grant had curled up next to his daddy, the two of them sound asleep. April began to fuss, so he went in and picked her up, then changed her diaper before taking her downstairs. "Are you hungry?" he asked, taking her temperature with the back of his hand. She seemed fine, and he got her a little cereal and some juice, and once she was done, she climbed down from the table and found her shopping cart, then grabbed some of the furniture from the doll house to put in it. Maybe she was playing moving van. Anyway, she wheeled it around the house with Benjamin following her like she had liver snaps in her pocket.

Kevin sat at the table with a cup of coffee, wondering how he'd gotten drawn into this. A couple weeks ago he was this unattached and carefree firefighter, and with one decision, he was now a babysitter and caretaker for a two-year-old. Granted, her daddy was just upstairs. Before the apartment building fire, he had wanted kids, but he would never have thought that he'd have an instant family of sorts. It was a huge change, and he wondered if he was good enough for it.

"Toons," April said, pushing her cart up next to him.

"Sure, honey." Kevin got up and found a channel she liked on TV. April settled on one of the floor cushions with Benjamin on her lap, enthralled. Well, that was easy enough.

"I'm sorry," Willy said as he shuffled in, blinking, with his hair askew. "I gave Grant some Children's Tylenol, and he's sleeping for now. He has a fever, but I think the medicine is bringing it down. He's not as hot as he was a little while ago."

"Do you want to take him to the doctor?"

"I already called, and we have a video appointment later today. There doesn't seem to be much need to take him in at this point. I suspect it's something that's going around the daycare and he picked it up from one of the other kids." He flopped into one of the kitchen chairs, and Kevin brought him a mug of coffee. "You don't have to stay around here if you don't want to. I know sick kids aren't something you signed up for."

Kevin sat down in the chair next to him. "Hey. To be honest, I don't have a clue what I signed up for, as you put it. But we're sort of figuring things out. April had cereal for breakfast, and she's happy enough." He shrugged.

"I know. But it must suck to date someone like me. I mean, we're young, and most gay guys my age are going out, having fun, doing the horizontal hula with every guy they meet. They don't spend their days going to garage sales for toys and taking care of sick kids." He gently placed his hand on Kevin's cheek. "I'll understand if this is too much for you. I really will. You were kind enough to take us in and see us through a hard time, but… well… I'll understand." He stood and left the table with his mug of coffee. "I need to check on Grant." He hurried out of the room, and Kevin wondered what he'd done to deserve the brushoff. Was this Willy's way of telling him that they should just be friends and that was all he wanted? Kevin shook his head and wondered if he should just go.

Chapter 9

Grant was asleep when Willy checked on him. He carefully took his temperature, relieved that it was going down. The dogs watched him from their nest at the foot of the bed, and both followed him out of the room and back to the kitchen.

"Maybe I should just go. I don't want to be in your way, and…."

"You aren't," Willy assured him.

Kevin knitted his eyebrows together. "Then what was all that earlier?" His voice held a slight icy chill.

"I just don't want you to feel trapped by all this. It's a lot, and you're a nice guy and the kind of person who would stick around because you felt like you should, or something. And I want you to understand that I get it. This is a lot—*we* tend to be a lot—and…." God, he was rambling like some kind of idiot.

"Are you freaking out on me?" Kevin asked.

Willy shrugged. "I don't know. Maybe I am a little. After last night, things were… well, they were…." He felt his cheeks heating. "They were magical, but today reality came crashing back in, and I guess I figured that it might be too much. So I…."

"So you figured that if you gave me the little speech about being able to leave that it might soften the blow if that was what I wanted to do?" He shook his head. "That's kind of messed up."

"No, it isn't," he said with more force than he intended. "This is my life. Sick kids, daycare, diapers, you name it. It's all part of my life, and it will be for a long time to come. It doesn't come to an end. All it does is change over time. And I just don't want you to think that you have to stick around unless it's something you want to do. I'll understand if it's too much because there are days when it seems like it's too much for me. That's all."

Kevin seemed confused, tilting his head slightly. "You keep saying the same thing as though it's going to make more sense the next time through. I'm still not sure what you want."

Willy set down his mug. "I'm saying that what I want doesn't matter. It's what you want that counts. And I'll understand if all this"—he waved his hand around the kitchen with the Legos under the kickplate and plastic food in a cart in the corner—"doesn't fit into the picture of how you want your life to be."

"How about you let me worry about how my life is supposed to be? You seem so concerned about what I want and what I think my life should look like, but I'm more than capable of doing that for myself. So don't worry about it, okay?" He stood and lightly kissed Willy on the head. Then he got some bowls and gave the dogs their morning food. "I like spending time with you… heck, I look forward to it. Yeah, I get worried sometimes because I want to do what's right for everyone, especially the kids." Kevin hugged him.

"Daddy, can I have some papple dus?" Grant asked from behind him.

"Of course," Willy answered as he pulled away. He poured Grant a covered cup of juice and took him into the other room, where he got him settled on the sofa under a blanket. "Do you need anything else?"

Grant shook his head and sipped his juice, so Willy left him to watch television.

"Is he okay?"

"Yes. His fever is down, and as long as I can keep him quiet, we should be okay. It's Sunday, and thankfully I don't have anywhere that I have to be." He sat back at the table with his coffee. "How about you? I know that you have to go into work this afternoon. I suppose that after all this drama, it will seem like a relief."

Kevin rolled his eyes. "Drama? You haven't lived until you're in a fire station with six guys, all of whom think they're God's gift to the world. Add to the mix the women that the men are primping over and you have a recipe for more drama than a telenovela. So don't worry about it. Besides, Grant was sick. That happens with kids. I just hope I don't come down with whatever he has."

"You and me both. I have had more colds and sniffles in the last few years than I ever had before. Between the two of them, they bring home everything."

Growls sounded from the other room.

"Benjamin," Kevin called, "you leave the others alone." He pushed back the chair, and the dog jumped onto his lap, settling across his knees. "He may be the smallest, but he rules the roost—or at least thinks he does."

"The other two are curled up with Grant."

"Yeah, and this guy decided that he wanted to be king of the couch." Kevin petted him, and Benjamin settled down.

At least the kids were quiet for the moment, and that gave him a chance to breathe. "I need to get dressed and cleaned up."

"Go on. I'll watch the munchkins."

Willy stood, and Kevin tugged him between his legs. "Just relax and don't worry about everything. Grant is going to be fine. He's already feeling better, and April is content watching her cartoons. They'll be quiet for a little while, so take a good long shower. I've got this."

He smiled and leaned closer. "Thank you." Willy kissed him, and thankfully the kids were engrossed enough in what they were watching that they weren't paying attention to them. "I won't be too long." He hurried to his room, where he grabbed clothes for the day. Then he went to the bathroom and started the water. He wished that Kevin could join him. Hell, he bet Kevin was sexy as hell wet and slippery. But Willy was also grateful for a full fifteen minutes that he could shower without being interrupted.

Once he was done, he dried off and dressed before hurrying downstairs to find both kids on the sofa, one at each end, the dogs between them, and Kevin sitting in the chair, reading on his phone.

"Were you good while I was upstairs?"

"No," Grant answered. "The baby tried to take my juice."

"I not a baby," April countered, and they were off.

"That's no way for either of you to act," Kevin said, and both kids quieted immediately. "Grant, you've been sick, and April, you have your own juice. So it's quiet time now. You can watch TV or go upstairs and take a nap." It seemed neither of them wanted that, so they sat quietly on the sofa.

"Wow," Willy mouthed. That was impressive.

Kevin smiled and slipped his phone into his pocket. "I need to get the dogs home and then go on to work." He got up and came over to Willy for a kiss. "I'll be late tonight, and you need to get the kids up early and go to work. That is, if Grant is feeling better. So I'm not going to stop by after my shift, but I'll see you later in the week. I'm on shift for the next few days, so it means being pretty busy."

"Okay. Message me when you're home." That way at least he wouldn't worry too much. "And I'll talk to you soon." Willy hated that he wasn't going to get to see Kevin for a while, but maybe that was for the best. They had been living pretty closely for a while, and a little distance would probably do them some good. If nothing else, it would give him a chance to think a little about what was happening. Since they'd met, it seemed like they were a freight train barreling down the tracks, and maybe a few well-applied brakes could make things better. Not that he really had a clue.

"I'll message when I get off shift." Kevin kissed him, and the kids covered their eyes with their hands. Then Kevin called the dogs and all of them were off.

As soon as the door closed behind them, the house seemed quieter and emptier. Willy looked around, trying to figure out what he should do next. But he figured sitting down for a while wouldn't be too bad. Within ten minutes, he found himself thinking about Kevin. Within an hour, he was climbing the walls. The kids were quiet, and he should be grateful for the downtime, but all he wanted to do was get out and find something fun, like taking the kids to the park, but that was out. So instead he watched cartoons until his brains threatened to turn to mush. Then he read for a while… and every so often, he checked out front to make sure no one was watching the house.

WILLY WAS not sure if returning to their daily routine was a good thing or not, but it surprised him how easily they all fell into old patterns. He got the kids up, dressed, fed, lunches packed, and then off to daycare before he taught his classes and held office hours. The most shocking thing was how easily he fell down the rabbit hole thinking about Kevin. All it took was a few minutes of quiet time, or a damned committee meeting where everyone talked themselves hoarse and said nothing, for him to find himself wondering what Kevin was doing and if he was safe.

More than once, he replayed their night together in his head, but he had to stop that because it took him on a flight of heated fancy that left him warm and grateful for the table in front of him. At night he'd pick the kids up, make them dinner, and then let them play for a while before putting them to bed and fighting to get Grant to go to sleep. At the end of the day, he'd text Kevin, smile when he got an answer, and then go up to his own bed… and dream.

Bed was the one place he knew he could let his mind wander all he wanted. But by the time he collapsed, he was usually too tired to do anything about it. But the dreams—oh, they were wild, and he often woke covered in sweat and wished he was asleep once more.

By Friday, he was ready for the weekend. Fortunately he didn't have any classes and spent hours in his office with the door closed, grading examinations that proved he was doing a good job getting some pretty complex concepts across. He had bright students, and their determination came through in their work. He knew economics wasn't easy, but this particular class was doing very well.

A knock pulled him out of his work. He opened the door and then checked the clock.

"You've been in here all afternoon," Evelyn said as she stepped inside. She set a box on his desk. "This arrived for you, so I brought it up from the break room."

"What is it?" He only had a few more exams to grade, and he really wanted them done so he wouldn't have to finish them over the weekend. He looked at the box and pulled the note attached. "Is it from Kevin?" It certainly hadn't been sent through the mail.

"He asked me to deliver it when I saw you, but you've been sequestered in here all day, so I figured I'd better bring it to you."

Willy opened the box and immediately smelled a little smoke. He pulled off the tissue paper and gasped. "Where did he get this…?" He gently pulled out the small bronze dog. He checked it over, realizing it was his.

"This week, Kevin was able to get into your old building, and he found this in the basement in a pile of ash and debris. When Kevin told me, I said I expected it was yours. You had shown me a picture of it."

"Yeah. My grandmother used this as a doorstop." He stared in disbelief. The dog had been on a shelf in his living room, and he never thought he'd see it again. "And Kevin found it."

"Yeah. He wasn't sure how to go about cleaning it or anything, so apparently he brushed off the soot and pretty much left it. They've had him working long hours, so he asked me to bring it in for you." She smiled.

"I appreciate it so much." It was hard to describe how it felt to have this back. With everything else gone, it meant a great deal to have something of his past restored to him. Willy picked up his phone and sent Kevin a text with plenty of smiley faces. Kevin messaged right back with how happy he was. "But why didn't he give it to me himself?" He could feel the weight of doubt pressing on him.

"Well, they changed his schedule. One of the guys got injured on a call, and he's out for a few days. Kevin took one of his shifts to help cover, so he has to work tomorrow and Sunday, and he didn't want you to have to wait to get it." Even she sounded disappointed. "I know this is difficult."

"Yeah, it is. But it's the life of a firefighter. He helped us a lot, and there are other people who need him now." Willy shrugged as though he were making light of it, but he had been looking forward to seeing him all week, and between their schedules, they hadn't been able to manage anything.

"Hey, none of that. It's just part of the job and has nothing to do with how he thinks about you." She rolled her eyes. "Now I'm going to leave you to get back to work so you can pick up the kids." She patted his shoulder and then left the office.

Willy put the dog back in the box and set it aside. He figured he could clean it when he got home. He set about finishing the last of the exams and then grabbed the box and hurried out of the building to pick up April and Grant.

"WHAT DID you do today?" Willy asked once he had the kids buckled in their seats.

"Played dolls," April said, but Grant was unusually quiet.

"Grant," Willy prompted, "what did you learn?"

"That Tawan is a poopoo head and I don't want to talk to him no more." He crossed his arms over his chest. "He said I took his truck and I didn't and I told Miss Mary that I didn't and he said I did. But I didn't, and then Miss Mary found his truck in his bag and Tawan said I put it there so I wouldn't get in trouble after I took it, but I never took it." He sounded ready to cry.

"What did Miss Mary say?"

"That Tawan forgot his truck was in his bag and that it wasn't nice to call me a stealer. Tawan said sorry, but I know he didn't mean it." Grant and Tawan had an on-and-off friendship of sorts. Willy would be glad when Grant moved on next year. He'd be in preschool and Tawan would be staying in daycare because of a few happy months' age difference. A separation would do Grant good.

"Okay. Well at least he said sorry, and you can play with other kids, right?" Willy asked gently. He knew this was most likely a momentary blip and that by Monday the boys would be playing together again.

Grant said that he did and then told him all about the pictures he drew and that he played with a girl named Val and that apparently she was nice for a girl.

"I'm a girl," April said, to which Grant had no answer.

When they arrived home, Willy made them a snack of apples and peanut butter before checking his work email for the last time before the weekend. Then he sent Kevin a message, but he didn't receive an answer, so he pretty much knew he was on a call.

"Can we visit Kevin?" Grant asked. "I wanna play with the dogs."

"Me too," April echoed.

"Kevin is working right now, so he isn't home. But I can put on a movie for you. Which one would you like?"

"*Encanto*," Grant said as he got up from the chair, doing some kind of butt-wiggling dance.

"Belle," April said. "I want Belle." She began to sniffle.

"How about we watch *Beauty and the Beast* today and *Encanto* tomorrow?"

Grant sighed dramatically. "Fine. We can watch Belle."

"I love Belle."

Grant grinned. "I like Beast." He made roaring noises and continued his dance, which had changed to some sort of Beast dance, or at least that was what Grant said. Eventually Willy got the kids to finish their snacks and then put on the movie. While they watched, he cleaned the bathroom and straightened up in the kids' rooms. There was so little in the apartment, yet they managed to spread what there was everywhere. Once that was done, he went to get the box and brought it inside.

Everything smelled like smoke and ash, so he took the box outside and followed the directions on an art restoration website to clean the piece with a little gentle soap and water. Then he placed the dog on one of the largely empty built-in living room shelves.

"Is that our doggie?" Grant asked, running over to look at it. "Kevin's doggies are better. You know why? Because they're real and they can play and sleep with you and everything."

"Do you remember it?" Willy asked. "They found it after the fire." It was a little worse for wear, but the dog was in one piece. Grant nodded and then went back to watching the movie, which was great. Willy made a simple dinner and got everyone fed, pausing the movie so they'd eat. Then they wanted to finish it as soon as they were done. "Once the movie is over, you both need to have a bath and then get ready for bed." Both kids ignored him. "Did you hear me?"

He finally got two nods and went to check out front. Since that guy had shown up, Willy had been watching, but he hadn't seen anyone. Maybe it was because he hadn't been asking around or inquiring into the fire. He had been pretty vocal for a while, but maybe whoever had sent that guy thought they had gotten to him. Who knew? All that counted was that they were leaving him alone and the kids were safe. Maybe he should have called the police, but he didn't have much to tell them.

Willy closed the door and locked it before returning to the kids just in time for Belle to tell the Beast that she loved him just as the last petal of the rose fell. The kids were fascinated as the Beast rose into the air and transformed into the handsome prince.

"Okay, both of you. It's bath time and then bedtime." He ignored the chorus of protests and shooed Grant into his room and got April in the tub. She was not a play-in-the-water girl. April wanted to get in and get out, so he got her washed, rinsed, and wrapped in a towel to dry. Then he dressed her and put her to bed before getting Grant in for his bath.

He swore that kid would do anything to not go to bed, but eventually he got him bathed and in his PJs before putting him to bed with a story. "Now go to sleep. Nothing is going to happen, I promise. You aren't going to miss anything. Go to sleep and we'll do something fun in the morning."

"Like what?"

"I don't know, but it's Saturday. We can go to the park and feed the ducks, and you and April can play on the playground, okay? So the sooner you go to sleep, the faster you get to do that." He gently rubbed Grant's back, and Grant settled under the covers. Finally he closed his eyes, and Willy left the room, closing the door most of the way. Then he quietly returned to the living room, shut off the light, and put on a murder mystery series from PBS.

Willy fell asleep during the second episode. When he woke, he was about to go to bed when someone knocked on the door. It was nearly midnight, but he checked through the window before opening the door to Kevin and the dogs, who raced inside. "I thought I'd take a chance that you would still be up."

Willy pulled Kevin inside, closed the door, and then kissed him as though the world were coming to an end.

"God, I missed you. The kids keep asking when they can come over to see you," Willy said as he broke the kiss, but Kevin held him tight.

"I missed you too, and I probably should have gone home to bed, but I wanted to see you, so I risked it." Kevin kissed him again. "I have to be back at seven in the morning, so I only have a few hours and then I have to be up again." He slowly placed Willy back on his feet.

"Then let me put down some water for the dogs," he said before heading to the kitchen, where he got a couple of plastic bowls and placed them on the mat near the back door. Then he took Kevin's hand and led him to the bedroom. "Go ahead and get into bed. I need to check on the kids and I'll be right back."

As he expected, Elsa was in her place at the foot of Grant's bed, and Benjamin with April, both of them already on guard. He smiled and returned to his room. Kevin had undressed and lay partially under the covers, his eyes closed. Willy turned out the light and got cleaned up before joining Kevin in bed. He pulled up the covers and rolled over toward him. But other than the rise and fall of the bedding, Kevin didn't move. He was already asleep.

Thumper jumped onto the foot of the bed and took his place as Willy got settled. He knew he needed to sleep, but having Kevin there made him stay awake just because he didn't want to miss anything. He took Kevin's hand, and without waking, he held Willy's back, and that was how Willy fell asleep.

WHEN WILLY woke the following morning, Kevin was gone and there was a note on the pillow next to him.

Sorry. I had to go, and I didn't want to wake you or the kids. I hope it's okay, but I left the dogs here for the day. They have been spending so much time alone, and I thought the kids would like the time with them. If that's a problem, I can swing by sometime and take them home. Hopefully I'll get off shift earlier tonight and we can make a little magic.

Kevin.

"Daddy, the doggies," April called as she came in the room and jumped up on the bed with Benjamin right behind her.

"Yes. Kevin brought them over, and they're going to stay with us today." She slipped under the covers and cuddled up against him. "Are you still sleepy?"

"No. Cartoons," she said, and Willy groaned. He wasn't ready to get up, but it looked like his day was starting now, whether he was ready or not.

"Okay. Go out and I'll be there in a minute to find some for you." There were days when he wished morning came just a few hours later. "But be quiet so you don't wake Grant, and I'll make pancakes for breakfast," he added in a whisper, and she jumped up and down before hurrying out of the bedroom. He supposed he was lucky she didn't forget and scream for joy.

Once Willy was dressed, he found April sitting on her floor pillow, staring at the blank television screen. He turned it on, found some cartoons, and kept the volume low. Then he went into the kitchen to mix pancake batter and put some bacon in the oven. He knew what the kids liked, and sure enough, as soon as the bacon scent escaped the kitchen, Grant hurried in, rubbing his eyes.

"Bacons?" he asked.

"Yes." He picked him up and swung him around. "Now go get dressed. I set out the clothes for you last night. Then when you get back I'll make the pancakes." That would be one dressed and up. He got April changed into Pull-Ups and dressed at just about the time the bacon finished cooking.

The dogs crowded into the kitchen when he got the kids in their chairs and started the pancakes. The entire place smelled amazing. He made up plates with a pancake each, along with two half pieces of bacon and a glass of juice. "You need to eat that. Don't feed it to the dogs." April was already breaking off a piece of her pancake with a gleam in her eyes.

Grant dug in, and Willy cut up April's pancake so she could eat it easily. Everything was such a production. He finally managed to get his own pancakes and sat at the table to eat. Just as he took the first bite, his phone rang. Willy didn't recognize the number and almost didn't answer it, but after a couple of rings, he picked it up.

"Willy, it's Chase."

"Is Kevin all right?" he asked, intuiting a calamity.

Chase hesitated. "He will be. But we were at a house fire and Kevin was inside to bring out the last person when the ceiling collapsed on top of him. He managed to get out, but he's been taken to the hospital. I thought you would want to know."

"I do. Thank you. Does he have his phone?"

"No. It's at the station. When we're done here, I can bring it over to him."

Willy ate more quickly. "Thank you. I'll get the kids in the car and we'll head over to check on him." His stomach clenched, and he pushed the plate away.

"Okay. We're still at the scene here. They took him by ambulance about ten minutes ago."

"I'll call you when I get there and find out how he is." Willy ended the call. "Kids, you need to finish up and we need to go. Kevin has been hurt, and we need to go to the hospital and make him feel better."

"'Kay," Grant said and stuffed the last of his breakfast in his mouth, holding some of it in his cheeks like a chipmunk. Once he swallowed and April was done, they got in the car and Willy drove as quickly as he dared through town.

CHAPTER 10

KEVIN HURT all over. His left arm and neck ached, and he knew he'd been burned, but not too badly, thanks to his fire suit. But damn, it was like he had been hit by a truck. What really bothered him was his breathing. The ceiling collapse had taken out his breathing gear, so his lungs ached if he took a deep breath.

Clair had gotten him out. They didn't often work together, but she was tough as nails and a great firefighter. She hadn't hesitated to pull him out and had gotten him on his feet and to safety. Once he'd been taken to the ambulance, he lost track of what was happening with the fire, but that was okay. The other firefighters would do their jobs and make sure the scene was safe.

"How is your breathing?" a nurse asked him when she came in.

"It's okay," he said. They had him on oxygen, and he was getting enough air. What concerned him was the way his lungs felt tight when he took a deep breath, and he told her what he was feeling.

She checked all the monitors and the IV that they had given him. "Is it feeling any better over time, or about the same?" He started to speak but had a coughing spasm and closed his eyes. Then, once it passed, he slowly took a deep breath again. This time the tightness came later and wasn't as bad.

"I think it's getting better," he told her.

"Good. Just relax and give your system a chance to deal with what happened. You had a close call." She pulled out a tray and began checking over his arms and neck. "You got a few small burns, and I'm going to clean and dress those, but if you ask me, you were pretty lucky."

"Yeah, I was. My partner did a great job getting me out. Clair is a real badass." He felt a cough coming on but relaxed and the sensation passed. "Am I going to be okay? I still have the rest of my shift."

"I think you're going to be here for a little while." She worked on his wounds, and he closed his eyes and let her do her thing. They needed to be tended to, but he needed to get back to the station so he could do his job. Lying here in a bed was not helping anyone. She finished up and was about to leave. "The doctor will be in soon to talk to you." She flashed him a smile and then left his room.

"Shit," he swore, half under his breath. He should have been more careful, but the ceiling hadn't looked that bad. Then, damn, it just all came down on top of him. He had been lucky in that there must have been water soaking it from the other side, because the weight did more damage than the actual on-fire part had. Still, he felt like a fool for allowing this to happen. But there was nothing he could do about it now, so he closed his eyes and tried to relax.

"Here he is," a familiar voice said, and Willy came in the room with April and Grant each holding a hand.

"Are you okay?" April asked, letting go of her daddy's hand and coming right up to the bed. She then took Kevin's hand. "Do you have an owie?"

"Yes, I do. But they're trying to make it better," Kevin told her. "I promise."

"Really?" Grant asked. "Did they bring you in an ambulance? Did you get to run the sirens?"

Kevin chuckled but stopped when coughs threatened. At least taking deeper breaths was getting easier. He took another one and closed his eyes, relieved that the tightness seemed to be dissipating.

"Chase called me and we hurried over," Willy said from next to him. "How is your breathing? What are they worried about?"

"That he'll act like firefighters usually do and try to go back to work too danged soon," Dr. Rosco Mortimer said as he walked into the room.

Kevin and Rosco had crossed paths quite a few times over the years.

"Don't tell me you aren't thinking about how you can go back to work. Just know, it's not happening."

"But Rosco—" Kevin began, but he knew it was useless when he got that look.

"Your lungs took in a lot of soot. You're lucky your partner got you out of there as quickly as she did or it would have been a lot worse." He used the stethoscope to listen to Kevin's lungs and heart. "It's better than it was when you came in, but that doesn't mean you're out of the woods."

"So what now?" Kevin asked.

"I'm going to send you home, but you need to rest. Do you have someone to look after you?"

"Kevin is going to come home with me and the kids. We'll look after him. His dogs are already there, and I'm sure they'll stand guard and make sure he takes it easy. He can sit on the sofa with the kids and watch cartoons. It's Grant's turn to pick today, so Kevin can watch *Encanto* until he passes out."

"Good," Rosco said with a smile. "He needs someone to look out for him or else he'll go running into burning buildings." Rosco was teasing, and Kevin thought about flipping him the bird, but he remembered the kids were there, and he did not want to have to explain that to them.

"How long before he can go?" Willy asked.

"I want a picture of his lungs, so they're going to do a CAT scan. Someone will be in to take him down in a few minutes. Once those results come back, he should be good to go." Rosco left the room, and soon Kevin was on his way down for tests. April wanted to ride along, but she stayed behind with Grant and a concerned-looking Willy.

BY THE time Kevin got back, Willy was sitting in a chair in the room with April on his lap and Grant on the floor, spread out on his belly, coloring. "How did it go?" Willy asked.

"Oh, it was peachy, but I hate that. It makes me claustrophobic—and I go into burning buildings for a living." The orderlies put the bed back into place, and April climbed into the bed with him.

"Be careful, honey," Willy said, but Kevin made room for her, and she settled next to him.

"Did they fix your owie?" April asked and then went off about her last owie, showing him where it had been and telling him that it was all better because Daddy kissed it. Kevin tickled her a little, and she giggled. He was quickly becoming addicted to the happiness that radiated from Willy's small family.

"How is your breathing?" Willy asked. "Is it better?"

"Yeah. That seems to be working its way out pretty well." At least he could breathe without the tightness. That was good. Willy held his hand, and they sat quietly for a while until Rosco returned with the news.

"You got really lucky. Your lungs are largely clear, but there are areas where you got material into them. But it appears that your system is expelling it. You need to rest and let your lungs heal and your system take care of itself. I'm going to send a message to your regular doctor to have him see you in a week or so."

"When can I go back to work?" Kevin asked.

"You need rest and time to heal up. Give yourself some time. I'll send a message to the station so they know." Rosco drew closer to the bed. "And I mean it. Don't think about going back early because you're feeling better. Working with breathing equipment is going to be harder while you're recovering."

"We'll all watch him," Willy said. "And you need to do what the doctor says. All of us want you to heal up well."

Kevin growled. He hated being laid up and everyone knew it, especially Rosco.

"It's okay. You can stay with us for a few days, and we'll make sure you get taken care of." Willy put his hand on his shoulder, and Kevin closed his eyes and placed his own on top of it.

"Are you sure?"

Willy leaned over him. "Of course I am. You took care of us when we needed it, and we'll take care of you." He lifted his gaze. "How soon can we take him home to get him settled? And I need to know how much activity he can have."

"Walking outdoors as long as the weather is good, but he's not to overdo it. Though I'm sure he will want to run a marathon next week."

"Actually, it's the week after," Kevin quipped and then began coughing. Willy held his hand until the spasm passed. "Okay, I get it."

"You will cough, and you need to keep an eye on it. If you cough up blood, come right back in here. We need to see you immediately. Also, if the cough gets worse or you have any trouble breathing, don't wait to see if it gets better, okay?" Rosco was firm and stared at Kevin as a nurse came in the room with Kevin's phone.

"A Chase dropped this off for you, but he got called away," she explained.

"Thanks," Kevin said softly. The nurse nodded and left the room.

Kevin rolled his eyes at Rosco, but Willy agreed for him. "You can count on it." He squeezed Kevin's hand. "I want him to be around, and he needs to take care of himself." He'd hoped the interruption would have changed the subject.

Kevin's first instinct was to be pissed, but then he looked at Willy and saw only concern and care. It had been quite a while since anyone felt that way about him.

"Okay. I think I got this." He lay back. "Can we get on with it?"

"Sure. I'll have one of the discharge coordinators come in with the paperwork. But I want to warn you, you shouldn't be alone for the next few days in case something happens, so spend some time with your family and enjoy it. The work will be there when you get back. It isn't going anywhere." Rosco left the room, and April shifted next to him.

"Can we get food? I'm hungry."

"Can we go to the park to feed the ducks, like you said?"

Willy chuckled. "Yes, we can go do all those things, but we have to take it easy on Kevin."

"Yes, we can do that. Now why don't you let your daddy lift you down so I can sit up and be ready when they spring me from this chicken coop? Then we can go do something fun. I don't think I can play with you, but I can probably sit and watch."

The nurse came in, and Kevin signed everything he needed to, then took the papers. Willy followed the orderly as he wheeled Kevin out of the hospital and to his car. Kevin got inside while Willy buckled the kids in before they took off.

"Are you hungry?" Willy asked, and Kevin nodded. "Okay, then. What do you want?"

"Soup and maybe some bread or something. They gave me stuff for the pain, and I don't want to upset my stomach."

"Okay. I know where to go. The Hamilton downtown makes their own soup, and they have plenty of things the kids will eat. Then after lunch we can go to the park, as long as Kevin is feeling okay."

Willy found a parking spot right in front of the restaurant, and they all went inside and got a booth. Willy ordered for himself and the kids, while Kevin got the soup and sat back and closed his eyes.

"I guess you're tired. Maybe we should take you home."

Kevin shook his head. "The kids can play at the park and feed the ducks. It's supposed to rain tomorrow, so they should have fun today." He got comfortable, trying to relax, but all he saw and felt was the ceiling collapsing on top of him again and again. He ate slowly and did his best to stay engaged, but his mind kept going over what happened. "I should have—"

"No," Willy said forcefully, leaning over the table. "You don't get to second-guess everything you did a million times and try to figure out what you missed. This happened, and you know that fire is unpredictable. That's why you go in with someone else."

Kevin's eyes widened.

"I read a lot on the internet about what you do. Clair was there because she was supposed to be. It was her job to back you up just like you backed her. So this coulda, woulda, shoulda stuff is a waste of time and effort. Now please eat your soup and relax. You're here with us, and that's what really counts. Okay?"

Kevin snickered. "You should be a therapist. You could get your patients in and out of your office in a single session."

"You don't need to pick on me. Or else I won't share my fries with you, and these are really hot and fresh, so you'll be missing out on really good stuff." He grinned, and Kevin nicked a fry from his plate.

"Okay." He ate it and then finished his soup, and felt better by the time he was finished. "So what were your plans for today before I interrupted?"

"The park with the swings and the ducks," Grant told him. "Daddy was going to take us so we can play." He ate his hot dog with a grin. "Can the dogs come play with us?"

"Yeah," April added, bouncing in her booster seat.

"How about we go to the park after we eat, and then we can go home and you can play with the dogs in the backyard?" Willy looked tired, and Kevin figured he wanted to get home too. "Kevin is going to need to rest."

"O-kay," Grant said, as though the weight of the entire kid world was on his shoulders. He went back to eating, and Willy did the same as Kevin watched everyone, glad to be a part of this little group.

"Do you want some help?" Kevin asked April, and he cut up her hot dog in small pieces. She used her fingers to put some in her mouth. "Be sure to chew well." He made exaggerated chewing motions using another fry he nabbed from Willy's plate. He didn't want to explain how many hot dogs he had seen the paramedics Heimlich from choking kids. "You're such a big girl."

"No. She's the baby. I'm the big brother," Grant said.

"I not a baby," April protested, sticking her tongue out.

"That's enough, both of you. Behave or you won't go to the park," Willy told them without raising his voice. He was always so patient with the kids. "Now finish your lunch and be nice."

"But I not a baby," April said again from next to Kevin and then began to cry. Kevin put his arm around her.

"Hey. You're getting to be a big girl, so you can stop crying and finish your hot dog. Remember, the duckies are waiting." She looked up at him with big, watery eyes but went back to her lunch. Thankfully Grant left his sister alone, and they finished lunch quietly before paying the bill and piling back into the car.

Willy drove to the park, and as soon as he got the kids out of the car, they ran toward the playground at full speed. "You go watch them," Kevin said. "I'm going to put the window down and relax." He didn't want to stop them from having fun, but the pain medication was wearing off, and he felt like he had been beaten up by three clowns and their VW Beetle. None of the pain was acute, he just ached all over. Kevin took a couple of the pills Rosco had given him for pain, put the seat back, and waited for it to kick in.

Laughter drifted in through the open window, and he concentrated on the happy sound, trying not to play the incident through his mind again. Willy was right. He wasn't going to help himself by second-guessing everything. He was okay, and Willy was looking after him.

"Do you want to see the ducks?" April asked from outside his window.

"You all go," he said gently.

"Shhh," Willy told her as he lifted her up. "We need to let Kevin rest." He zoomed her away.

"Do me next," Grant said, and their voices faded as they crossed the park road toward the stream with its ducks and geese.

Kevin's phone vibrated in his pocket, and he fished it out and put it on speaker. "Hello." He didn't want to open his eyes. Maybe the painkillers were kicking in.

"Kevin…."

"Captain. I'm okay. No permanent damage, but Rosco told me I needed some time to let my lungs heal. I should be back in three or four days. He gave me some of the good stuff."

"I get that. Call in a few days to let us know you're okay. Where are you staying?" he asked. "You're not home alone, I hope."

"I'm with Willy," he answered. "I'll call you in a few days." He ended the call and kept his eyes closed. The pain had receded, and exhaustion had settled in. He just let himself relax and dozed off, waking when Willy put the kids in the car, and then they were off again.

He woke enough to get inside, with Willy guiding him into bed. "Rest well, and I'll check on you in a little while." He leaned over the bed and kissed him. "You gave me a real scare. Don't do that again." Willy's touch lightly trailed down his arm. Kevin opened his eyes and took Willy's hand.

"I didn't do anything wrong. I didn't know the ceiling was going to fall."

Willy leaned over him once more. "I know that. I just hate that you're hurt. It scared me when Chase called, and I raced to the hospital. So take care of yourself, rest, and get better." He kissed Kevin once more, this time harder than the last time. "I hope that sends you into dreamland with some happy thoughts."

It did.

CHAPTER 11

WILLY STAYED out back with the kids for much of the afternoon, letting them run off their energy. They seemed to have an endless supply of it, but once it got close to dinnertime, he got both kids inside and made a simple dinner. Just as he got the two of them at the table with their plates, a knock called him to the front door.

"Hey, Chase," he said as he let him in.

"How's Kevin?" he asked quietly.

Willy turned to the closed bedroom door. "He's still asleep. Whatever he took knocked him out hours ago. I checked on him, and he's sleeping hard, so I don't want to interrupt him. But I'm concerned that if I don't get him up for a little while, he'll be up all night." He closed the door and led Chase through to the kitchen. "What's up?"

"The fire today… it was set the same way that someone used to burn down what was left of your building."

Willy offered him some dinner, but he declined. "I guess mac and cheese isn't your thing." He smiled. "It's not mine either, but these two munchkins like it." He hated the stuff, but he wasn't going to argue when the kids wolfed it down.

Chase nodded. "The thing is, the building that burned today, the one where the ceiling came down on him…."

Willy pulled out the chair. "Let me guess. It was built by the same people who did the apartment building."

Chase nodded.

"And since it was built for sh… badly, the ceiling came down on Kevin." Whoever was behind all this, Willy wanted to smack the living hell out of them. "Do you know what else they built in town?"

"That's just it. They built a few things and then they were gone. It was a short period of time, and then I guess word got around that they were doing crappy work and they went back to Philly. But whatever they built, they seem to be willing to put people's lives in danger to try to cover it up."

Willy nodded. "This is more than building code violations. It has to be. Why put a bunch of people in danger for something like that after all these years? Something else is going on."

"What something else?" Kevin asked as he padded out of the bedroom, beautifully disheveled in Willy's robe.

"Uncle Kevin," Grant said as he jumped up from the table and raced over to him. Kevin humphed as Grant slid to a stop, his arms around his legs. "Are you better now?"

"I will be." He caught Willy's gaze, looking a little confused.

"While you were sleeping, we decided that Uncle Kevin was what the kids would call you instead of just using your name. It's more respectful." Willy loved the surprised and pleased expression.

"Why don't you finish your dinner and we can play Legos afterwards."

Grant returned to the table, and Willy guided Kevin to the sofa and covered his legs with a dinosaur throw blanket he'd gotten at Target at Grant's insistence.

"What's going on?" Kevin asked, looking up at him and Chase.

"That fire you got injured in was intentional," Willy said, bringing Kevin up to date. "And the building was built—"

"By our friends at Kraft and Hobson," Kevin supplied.

"Yeah."

"I was just saying that there's more to this than some building code violations," Willy added. "These buildings were built over a decade ago. There's no way that anyone could go after them for these kinds of things. Statute of limitations and all. So there has to be something else."

"Like what?" Kevin asked.

Willy shrugged. "I don't know. You're the firemen. I'm an economics professor. But if you want to know something, I suggest you follow the money. That drives a lot of what people do. People lie, cheat, steal, and kill for money, so why not set a few fires?"

"Okay. But it wasn't like they would get money from insurance or anything," Chase offered. "They don't own the buildings, they just built them."

Willy had no idea, and it seemed the rest were as baffled as he was. "I don't think we're going to come up with any answers staring at each other. Maybe think on it."

"I need to check on the permits and inspections of this latest building. Maybe there's something there." Chase stood, fist-bumping Kevin. "I hope you feel better soon, and I'll let you know if I find anything." He left, and Willy locked the door behind him.

"Can we play Legos now?" Grant asked as he hurried into the living room with the dogs behind him.

"Sure," Kevin told him. "Go get them and we'll see what we can build." Kevin sat back, and Willy wondered if this was a good idea. "I'm going to be fine. It's just a little while." He must have read Willy's expression.

"Don't let him wear you out," Willy told him and helped April down. Then he put on a movie for her, and she sat entranced on her floor pillow, Benjamin sitting in her lap. The other two dogs took up places on the sofa on either side of Kevin, while Willy grabbed a book he had been wanting to read and sat in the chair to enjoy a quiet evening at home.

The letter box beside the door snapped closed, making him jump a little. It was late for the mail. He got up and found a piece of paper on the floor. Wary, he picked it up and read it, nearly dropping it back to the floor.

"What is it?"

Willy refused to play whatever game the asshole who'd already tried to threaten him was playing. "It seems our friend from the other day has decided to leave us notes. 'Back off or else!'" He showed it to Kevin and then set it aside. He didn't want to let it bother him, but it did. What if he decided to burn him out again? "He must really be desperate." The fear was so real, but he knew he couldn't let it get the better of him or this asshole would win.

"Aren't you upset?" Kevin asked.

Willy shook his head, but he knew it was a lie to appear strong. "I kicked his...." He caught himself before swearing. "I took care of him once. I'll do it again." Damned cowards. He refused to let that man get to him and ruin their quiet time. Willy sat back down and picked up his book once more, forcing himself to read, but he barely saw the words.

"THAT'S QUITE an ordeal," Kevin said once April and Grant were in bed. "Does it get easier?"

"Sometimes. Grant never wants to go to bed because he's afraid he'll miss something fun, so he tries to stay awake. April usually goes to bed easily, but she was on a tear. Thankfully they are both asleep, and I hope they stay that way." Willy sat on the sofa next to Kevin, shooing Thumper out of the way. "How is your breathing?"

"It's okay. I'm still coughing some, but not as much as I was earlier. Everything still aches, but I know that's going to pass fairly quickly. The pain meds work, but they make me loopy and weird. And of course I slept all day, so I'm wide awake now."

"Then we can put on a movie," Willy suggested before turning down the lights. "Just relax." He was grateful for a little quiet time. "What sort of movie would you like?"

"I don't know. Something calm and kind of quiet. A little fun."

Willy pulled up Netflix and found a rom-com set around a wedding in Thailand. It sounded fun and had some nice-looking guys in it. Then he got comfortable and settled down to watch.

About halfway through the movie, Willy paused it and got them both something to drink and a bag of chips. He brought them in and restarted the movie.

"I keep wondering what could be behind these fires."

Willy leaned against Kevin's arm as though this were the most normal conversation, rather than a discussion of the motives for arson. "I know. I'm watching the movie, and I keep expecting the entire resort to go up in flames at any moment. It's kind of a buzzkill."

Kevin chuckled. "Welcome to my world. Every time I go to the theater or a restaurant, I wonder what would happen if the place caught fire, how I'd get everyone out. It really kind of sucks. I can't turn it off. Like I know that if something happened here, there are two doors and we'd get the kids and dogs out in a matter of seconds. I also know which windows we could escape from. It's maddening, and yet…."

"Sort of comforting in a way," Willy offered. "After the fire, I looked at the same sort of things. There are three fire extinguishers in this place, one in the kitchen, another in the closet right over there, and there's one in the linen closet near the bedrooms. I wondered if that was enough, but maybe a fire extinguisher in the bathroom is going a little bit too far." He chuckled. "Still, why would someone want to burn down buildings that they built unless they did something really wrong?" Willy sighed and closed his eyes. "I'm on a hamster wheel, just going in circles with not enough information to get me anywhere. And I hate it because I want answers, just like you do."

"Yeah, I know. But I don't think we're going to get any through my usual channels," Kevin said softly. "We're going to need some help."

"What kind of help?"

Kevin put an arm around him. "Police help. We regularly share information with the local departments because arson investigations involve law enforcement. And I've worked with a couple of officers on the local force before."

Willy nodded. "Me too. I had some things stolen out of my storage location a few years ago. I never kept much in there after that. Anyway, the officer was very understanding, and I have his name somewhere. It was Carter… something."

"His partner is Red." Kevin leaned over and smiled. "At least his work partner. They're both really good officers. I have a number for them at the station, but I'll call the department in the morning and ask to speak to one of them. They understand these kinds of cases."

"If you say so," Willy said. "I just want all of this over with so we can all go back to our lives."

Kevin cleared his throat. "You do know that for me, this never stops. There is always another fire, another call, and sometimes another arson. It happens, and it's my job." He tugged Willy closer. "You and the kids are safe here, and you can begin to rebuild your lives. The insurance company should come through with payment because you had nothing to do with the fire."

"They said it should be soon."

"Good. Once they do, you can replace what you had and fill this place with everything you and the kids need." Kevin paused. "I guess I need to know if you want to be part of the ritualized chaos that is my life. I will always work odd shifts and get called in when really bad shit happens. I'll be one of the guys who runs into burning buildings. That isn't going to stop."

Willy swallowed hard. "I know that. Because you're a hero. And you have to know that I will sit at home and worry about you." He turned to look into Kevin's eyes. "So you better know that part of your job is to phone me after every damned call and let me know that you're okay. Don't make me get another call from Chase. Unless you're dead or unconscious, you damn well better call me, because if you don't, then

I'm going to think you're one of those two things. Understand?" He was as serious as a heart attack.

"I got it. As soon as I get out of a burning building, drop whatever I'm carrying and call you." Kevin smirked, and Willy lightly smacked him on the shoulder.

"Don't be a smartass. You can carry the people you rescue to the ambulance… and then call me." He met those warm eyes. "I could put together a set of rules and laws that we live by. After all, I'm an economist. I love lists and theoretical rules that may or may not reflect the actual world." He cocked his eyebrows at Kevin.

"Now I'm scared," Kevin whispered and drew closer.

"You should be. I can be a real terror when I get into list mode. I can organize everything and everyone to within an inch of their lives."

Kevin drew even closer, the television forgotten. "If that's true, then what's the first thing on your list?"

Willy didn't hesitate for a second and reached for the remote. "Turning off the television. Then we get you into bed, because you were in a fire today."

Kevin let his hands slide around Willy's waist. "And what do we do after that?" He slid them to Willy's lower back.

"Well, we don't do whatever you're thinking at this moment, because a certain sexy firefighter has lungs that aren't up to full capacity. And as hot as he is, there is nothing sexy about a coughing fit in the middle of boom-chicka-mow-mow." Willy rolled his hips just a little and then giggled.

"I think I hate your list." Kevin did his best imitation of one of Grant's pouts.

"Love it or hate it, the list is the list, and it's God. So come on. We need to get you into bed so you can rest and get better. You'll be off work for a few days, and the kids go to daycare on Monday. I can probably arrange to have my afternoon free." His blue eyes actually grew wicked.

"Damn." Kevin groaned, and just as he leaned close, his body betrayed him and he started coughing. "I was going to argue." He got himself under control, and Willy helped him to his feet.

"Let's get you in bed and you can rest. Tomorrow we'll get you some clothes and stuff from your house."

"Okay," Kevin agreed, and Willy let him use the bathroom first. Then he got Kevin into bed and checked on the kids, who were safe with their personal canine guardians. Then he got into bed after shooing Thumper down to the foot.

"He always was a bed pig," Kevin said, talking about the dog.

Willy snickered. "The real bed pig is the guy next to me. I swear you spread out across the entire bed in the night." He lightly patted Kevin's chest. "Go to sleep, and do your best not to push me out of bed, okay? I'd really appreciate it."

"Is that another thing on your list?" Kevin asked.

Willy sat up and leaned closer. "That's on a very special list that only you get to know about. So you go to sleep and I'll think about telling you what else is on that list, but only when you're feeling better." He shifted closer, letting his arm rest over Kevin's chest. "Just relax and go to sleep, because no matter what, as soon as it gets light, one of the kids will be up and raring to go."

"But tomorrow is Sunday." He sounded almost affronted at the idea.

"And to a two-year-old, it's just another day with an entire world to explore and grown-ups to do her bidding." Willy got comfortable and closed his eyes, hoping to all hell that he wasn't scaring Kevin off for good. Grant and April were amazing kids, and he wouldn't trade them for anything in the world, but they could be a lot, and he worried that Kevin was going to wake up and realize that they just weren't worth all the hassle.

WILLY WASN'T sure what time it was, but in the morning, he woke alone. The door was closed, and even the dog was gone. He got up, stretched, and checked the time, nearly panicking when he saw it was after eight. The kids never slept this late. He pulled on some clothes and hurried out of the room, only to find Kevin and the kids on the sofa in the living room. Kevin sat in the middle, with April and Grant on either side, all of them watching a movie about a man with a pet penguin. They all seemed enthralled.

"Did they eat?"

"We had cereal," Grant said with a smile, leaning against Kevin like he was a great big muscly pillow. April sat on the other side of him, her hand on Kevin's arm as she watched.

"Okay, then…," Willy said softly, leaving them to their television watching. All three dogs followed him into the kitchen, and he filled their water dishes. "Did you feed the dogs?"

"Yes," Kevin answered, so Willy gave them all pets and set about making an egg sandwich for himself. But it seemed Kevin wanted one as well, and Willy was smart enough to make him two, because he ended up sharing with the kids, who adored the things. It was so cute as Kevin held the sandwich and each kid took a careful bite. Damn it all, he could fall in love with the man just for how he cared for his children.

Willy brought each of the kids a juice box and then settled in the chair for his breakfast. He had three dogs all positioned around him, tails wagging as they watched every bite he took.

"They're better than any vacuum cleaner ever made," Kevin said as he finished his breakfast and set the plate on the coffee table.

Willy had things to do, so once he finished eating, he left them to their movie and took a few minutes to change the bedding for all of them and get the dirty sheets in the washing machine.

Once the movie was over, so was the reprieve. The kids went out to play in the yard as Willy did his best to finish his Sunday chores.

"What are you doing?" Kevin asked from right behind him.

"Loading the dishwasher."

"I think I like you like this," Kevin whispered. He ran his hand down Willy's arm before lightly squeezing his butt.

"I bet you do. But you aren't up for anything athletic yet." Willy straightened and turned around. "And if I'm honest, I don't dream of having sex in the kitchen. It just doesn't do it for me." He smirked. "Now, if you can figure a way for us to sneak away… I always dreamed of… well, under the stars has been a real fantasy for me."

"Okay. I'll see what I can do," Kevin said and then coughed hard. "Shit."

"Uncle Kevin said a bad word," Grant called from the back door. "Are you going to wash his mouth out with soap? That's what a lady on television did." He looked so danged cute, yet Willy knew he was full of mischief.

"How about a swear jar?" Willy offered. He had dreams about what Kevin did with his tongue, and none of it had anything to do with soap. "Whenever someone says a swear, they have to put a dollar in…." He opened the cupboard and pulled down a plastic container. "This." He opened the lid and held it out to Kevin. Grant crowed as Kevin put in a dollar, and then Willy closed it. "Go back outside."

"But I wanna listen for more swears."

"Scoot," Willy told him, and Grant went out to play. "You know he's going to listen to everything, and he'll make you pay."

"What will you use the swear jar money for?" Kevin asked. "I vote for beer, since I'll be the one paying. I just know it."

"Nope. I'm thinking ice cream this summer when it really starts getting hot. That seems fair to me." He went back to his chores, and Kevin sat down. "You're watching my butt, aren't you?"

"You said a swear." And just like a Grant-in-the-box, he was back.

"No, I didn't. *Butt* is not a swear. Now go sit on your butt outside or you can go upstairs and take a nap."

Grant's shoulders sagged as he returned to the backyard.

"Man, you're strict."

"There are real swear words, and I am not paying a buck every time I say *butt*. Now the other word is another thing. And we can say that all we want once we're in my bedroom and the door is closed. In fact, the swear jar is off once the bedroom door closes." Willy closed the dishwasher and started it.

"You're still tired."

"Yeah, I am. At least you didn't hog the bed last night. Your dog did that." He yawned and sat at the table with his second cup of coffee. Willy really needed something to wake him up.

"How about I get one of the Lego sets and Grant and I can put it together? That will give him something fun to do. And maybe you can do something with April." That sounded fine to him.

"DADDY," GRANT said as he and April come in from the backyard. They'd had a tea party on the patio, and April was happily carrying her dolls. "Kevin is sleeping." He sat at the coffee table with all the blocks in a huge pile, making something with great concentration. "I was being quiet."

"That's awesome. Thank you," Willy said and let Grant play. He wondered if Kevin was playing possum, but he went over and straightened the blanket. Sleep was the best thing for him, and Grant was playing fine on his own. Willy motioned Grant over. "What do you want for lunch?"

"Cheesy sandwiches," Grant said, and April nodded her agreement, so grilled cheese it was.

"Go ask Kevin if he wants one too. But do it quietly."

Grant was so serious. Willy peeked as Grant went in and right up to the sofa. "Uncle Kevin, Daddy wants to know if you want cheesy sammiches. And he says to be quiet." Of course he talked at his normal tone, which was loud enough to wake the dead. Willy went back into the kitchen so he didn't laugh in front of Grant.

"Tell your daddy that I would like one, please," Kevin said.

"Daddy, Uncle Kevin wants a sammich," Grant called before sitting back down and returning his attention to his blocks as though he hadn't just yelled through the entire apartment.

"I tried," Willy told himself and got out the bread, butter, and cheese. He also got some fruit and began cutting it up for a side dish.

A knock sounded on the front door.

"I'll get it," Kevin called, and he went to the door. "What the hell do you want?"

"He said a swear," Grant called, already racing for the container.

"I know. Just stay here," Willy said, holding Grant as Kevin let loose a few more choice words.

"You think we can't kick your ass into the middle of next week like we did the last time you showed up here? Making threats is a criminal offense. I'll call the police and make sure they have your description. Then you can deal with them." Kevin closed the door hard and whipped out his phone, coughing.

"What's going on?" Willy asked.

"Our friend paid you a visit. Apparently, getting his nuts handed to him wasn't enough." Kevin coughed some more before speaking to the police. "They're sending someone over."

"What did he want?" Willy asked, returning to the kitchen. No matter what drama was going on, he still had to feed the kids.

"Not sure. It's intimidation, but I have no idea what they think they can gain by this." Kevin sat at the kitchen table with a sigh. He coughed again, and Grant got up and began patting him on the back.

"Feel better?" he checked, and Kevin smiled at him and nodded.

"Much better. Thank you."

Willy got him a glass of water and placed it in front of him.

"I hate this cough."

"It's your body trying to get the gunk out," Willy said gently, then let Kevin relax. "What did the police say?"

The doorbell rang.

"I think I just got my answer." Willy answered the door and let in two officers, one familiar, and the other with a beard that partially hid the scar on his face.

"Hey, Willy," Carter said and shook his hand. "This is my partner, Red." Willy shook his hand as well. The guy was huge and would be intimidating without his smile.

"Kevin is in the kitchen." He led them through, and Grant hurried over to him, half hiding behind his leg as Willy lifted April into his arms.

"Are you a real policeman?" Grant asked. "Are you going to arrest Daddy?" He held him tighter.

"No. We're here to help your daddy," Red said. "And yes, we're real policemen. We help people when they need it. I promise."

"Let me get these two settled and we can talk." He got the kids on the sofa, the dogs surrounding them. Then he put on a movie. "I'll bring in your lunch." He was in the middle of way too many things. Once the movie was going, he returned to the kitchen to find Carter at the stove, flipping the sandwiches.

"I've made tons of these for Alex over the years," Carter said. He cut the sandwiches into quarters and put them on plates to cool a little.

"Is this some sort of full-service police force?" Willy asked, teasing.

Red sat down, and Willy joined him and Kevin. "What happened?"

"We've been visited twice by a man trying to intimidate us. The first time he threatened Willy, Willy laid him out on the sidewalk and left him singing soprano for a while. But the guy was back this morning. We don't know what he wants exactly, but his message was pretty consistent: leave things alone as far as Kraft and Hobson is concerned."

Carter brought over two plates for the kids and another with multiple sandwiches that he set on the table. Willy took the kids theirs, along with covered cups of milk. After making sure they were okay, he rejoined the others at the table. "Those sandwiches are for you, not the dogs," he called behind him, knowing exactly what was about to happen.

"Can you bring us up to date on the situation?" Carter asked, and Kevin provided background detail on the fires and the construction company.

"The thing is that Kraft and Hobson did shoddy work and likely defrauded their clients and the borough codes office. But that was over ten years ago. There isn't a lot anyone can do to them unless someone were to die. And so far no one has," Kevin said.

Carter made notes, and Willy grabbed half a sandwich and took a bite. "What I don't get is, why make threats at all? It's just going to get us to dig in. If they kept quiet, we wouldn't be here talking to you. I would have moved on, and the fire department would have done their job. Yeah, maybe Kraft and Hobson would have gotten some bad publicity, but it would have been minimal. There aren't real news sources any longer. The local papers don't get much circulation, so this is something that's going to go away very quickly for the most part."

"Exactly," Willy said. "It doesn't make sense."

"Can you give me a description of the man?" Red asked.

Willy nodded. "Black hair, scruffy, just below the ears, brown eyes, fake-tanned skin, dark stubble. This is a guy with constant five-o'clock shadow. He has a triangular-shaped face, and his nose was broken at some point. Maybe six foot or six-one. He's of decent build, but not bulky or too thin. His clothes were recent, not fancy but not too old either."

Red looked up from his notes. "Can I have you at all my crime scenes? Not that I want you to be a victim of a crime, but damn, if I got descriptions like this all the time, our jobs would be a lot easier."

Kevin placed his hand on Willy's. "I don't have anything to add after that. How did you get to be so observant?"

"I have two kids. How else can I keep my head above water and a step ahead of them?" He smiled. "When I was in high school, I wanted to be a police officer, so I watched every television cop show, and they all stressed how important it was to watch things. So I started playing games with my friends. We'd each write down questions, and at the end of the day, we'd answer them. It was a weird game. If the teachers had ever found our questions, they'd have been appalled. How big were Coach Johnson's pit stains after third period—stuff like that. We used to laugh over them, but I always won because I could recall just about everything during the day."

"And you did all that because you thought you might become a police officer?" Carter asked.

Willy chuckled. "Mostly because it was a fun away to get through the day. But good observation got me through college with top grades. What I really learned was to see what was there rather than what I expected to see."

Red nodded, and Kevin slipped his arm around Willy's waist. "What do you remember about when you first met me?"

Willy felt his cheeks color. "That you had your hand on my ass as you carried me."

"Daddy, you said a swear," Grant said as he ran in, the dogs behind him. He went to the counter and brought Willy the container. Willy got out his wallet and put in a dollar. Grant stretched to put the container back and returned to what he was watching.

"Okay, that was adorable," Carter said. "Alex used to do things like that when he was younger." He looked every bit the proud parent.

"Did you and your partner have him together?" Willy asked.

Carter shook his head. "Alex brought Donald and me together. We'd gotten off on bad footing. Donald works for Child Services and had a real reputation—"

"Because he will do just about anything to help the kids in his care," Red put in.

"Yeah. Red and I found Alex in an abusive situation. We rescued him, and caring for Alex was the catalyst for Donald and me. Alex is almost eleven now, and he remembers almost nothing from that time in his life. After Donald and I got married, we adopted Alex as our son. It was the best decision we ever made."

Willy nodded. "I don't know what I'd do without these two. Probably sleep more."

"But your life and your heart would be empty," Kevin said. "I know that." He took another half sandwich, and Willy did the same. The buttery cheesiness was amazing. American cheese was the worst, but in a grilled cheese, it was so good.

"So where do we go from here?" Willy asked. "I'm afraid for the kids. I have special instructions at the daycare that if anyone even asks after the kids, they are to call me. I don't want anyone to get to them."

"Carter here is great with computers. He'll use your description and a program we have to create a face. We'll send it to you so you can tell us how close we are, and once we have an image, we'll see if we can match it to anyone. The process can take a little time."

"Whatever I can do to support you," Willy said. "I want to get to the bottom of this. We've already lost our home and everything we had. The kids have been uprooted. The only good thing has been that we met Kevin in the deal. But putting everything back together…." He turned to Kevin. "I just want to feel safe again. I know it sounds dumb, but every time I hear a siren, I tense. I burned a piece of toast and nearly had a panic attack. I know it's going to take time for all that to pass. But… with all of it… it feels like it's just hanging on."

"We'll do everything we can," Carter said. "If he shows up again, call 911 and get through to the department. Say that this is a repeat attempt at intimidation and that you need someone right away. Use our names. But get someone here. Maybe we can catch him in the act."

"Yes, of course. We want that too," Kevin said.

"Are you living here now?" Red asked.

Kevin took Willy's hand. "I got caught in a fire, so Willy and the kids are looking after me. The hospital said they didn't want me to be alone." His smile told more of the story than Kevin provided.

Red nodded slowly. "Carter and I need to get going."

"Yes. I have plenty to do," Carter agreed. They both stood. "Expect an image later today."

"I'll watch for it," Willy said and showed both of them to the door. Once he saw them out, he checked around out of habit before closing and locking the door.

"Can we go to the park?" Grant asked.

"I don't think so. It looks like rain. But you can play here in the house. Go get your toys and play for a while." He figured April would be ready for a nap in an hour or so, and if he was lucky, he'd get Grant to be quiet for a while.

"I'm tired," Kevin said, yawning.

"Then go on in and get some rest." Willy would see to the kids and the dogs.

"Can we watch *Encanto*?" Grant asked, and Willy put the movie on. If Grant wanted to watch it again, then he could suffer through it, and Grant would stay glued to the movie until it was over. He got Grant settled on his pillow and sat on the sofa with April in his arms. She watched for a little while but got sleepy, and after maybe half an hour, he took her to her room and settled her in bed.

Now it was just Grant and him. Willy checked on Kevin, who was sound asleep with two of the dogs curled around him. Willy wished he could join him. The bed looked comfortable, and he wanted to slip in next to Kevin and hold him, but Grant needed him. He closed the door most of the way and found Grant in the living room, still glued to the movie.

"Come sit here with me," Willy said, and Grant climbed onto the sofa next to him. Willy turned the movie down, and Grant continued watching, but soon enough, he was asleep, and Willy took him in to bed as well.

A few minutes all to himself—that was a rare treat. He had plenty of chores to do, but he lay on the sofa instead, figuring he'd close his eyes for a few minutes. But soon his exhaustion caught up with him and he drifted off, only to wake quickly for no apparent reason. The house was quiet, the kids still asleep, the dogs all set, and even Kevin was snoring loudly enough to wake the dead.

Maybe everything was okay… at least for now. He'd been in crisis mode for too long, and it seemed strange not to have a million things pulling him in different directions. He sat on the sofa again, picked up his book from the table, and opened it. He tried to concentrate but put the book down again and just sat in his chair, staring at the wall. Willy knew something was going to happen—the man who threatened them would see to that. He just wished he knew what.

CHAPTER 12

AFTER THREE days, Kevin was still coughing and had no energy.

"You need to give yourself some time. You had a burning ceiling fall on you, and you're wondering why you can't just walk away as though nothing has happened. Think of it this way: you got some burns through your fire suit. Well, your lungs got some as well, and they need a chance to heal too."

"It's getting better, just not fast enough," Kevin groused, knowing he was complaining about something he could do nothing about.

The doctor pulled up a stool and sat down in front of him. "Look, I know you well enough to understand that sitting still is the last thing you want to do. You would rather run into a burning building than take a few days to rest and relax. But that is what you're going to have to do. I can't clear you for work when you're not ready to go back." He met Kevin's gaze with his caring one, but behind that care was absolute steel.

Kevin took a slow, deep breath and then let it out, pleased he didn't cough.

"If I let you go back and you went on a call and couldn't perform well, that would put others in danger. You know that."

"Shit, now you're using guilt?" Kevin knew the doctor was right; he was just getting impatient. It wasn't that he didn't like spending time with Willy. In fact, what was driving him crazy was that Willy and his little family had places to be and things to do, while Kevin had spent much of the days home alone now that the weekend was over.

"Whatever it takes." The doctor slid back and stood. "Give it some time and stop trying to push it. You're only going to make things worse."

"Fine. I was hoping you could give me a pill or some antibiotic or something to make me heal faster."

"Nope. You just have to wait like all the rest of us mortals." He chuckled. Kevin tried not to laugh but failed and ended up coughing and proving the doctor's point. "Go on home, rest, and give yourself some time. Looking at the tests run at the hospital, there is nothing that suggests you won't heal up naturally on your own." He stood at the computer station. "Now, if you don't continue to improve, then I want you to come back. And we'll make an appointment for two weeks to see how you're doing."

Kevin huffed but thanked the doctor anyway. He had thought he'd be off work for a few days, but it looked like it would be longer.

Kevin left the exam room and made the appointment on his way out before returning to his truck. He thought of going home. He had been at Willy's, but he knew he was getting in the way and didn't want to be another thing Willy had to take care of.

His phone rang, and he answered it through the Bluetooth.

"What did the doctor say?" Willy asked right away.

"That I need to give it time," he grumped. "I don't do sitting on my butt doing nothing very well."

"At least you admit it. That's the first step to recovery." Sometimes Willy was a real smartass.

"Har, har." Kevin pulled to a stop at a light at the north edge of town. "He says he wants to see me in two weeks. I thought it was only going to be a couple of days, and now…."

"It's okay. Just relax and try not to worry. You're getting better and have coughed less over the last few days, and I have no doubt it will keep improving." Voices carried through the line from behind Willy. "I need to go to class in a few minutes, but I'll see you at home in a few hours. Also, I got a call from Red. He asked if he and Carter could stop by this evening."

"All right. I'm going to stop by my place to pick up some fresh clothes, and I'll see you when you get home."

"Cool." Willy's smile came through in the brightness in his voice. "I'll see you then." He ended the call.

A few minutes later Kevin pulled up in front of his house and went inside. The rooms felt empty and almost too quiet. No dogs rushed up to meet him. They were still at Willy's, probably sprawled out on the sofa, taking a nap, waiting for April and Grant to come home. His dogs adored those kids. Kevin trudged upstairs and to his room and grabbed a bag out of the closet. He packed a few changes of clothes and then descended the stairs. This was his home, but right now it felt lifeless and empty. The thing was that Willy's place, even though it was bare and sparsely furnished, felt vibrant and full, humming with life all the time.

Without thinking about it too much more, he left. He thought about going right back to Willy's but detoured to the grocery store, where he walked the aisles, getting some things he knew Willy needed. By the time he reached the checkout, he was tired, winded, and coughing. Damn it all. A simple trip to the store should not feel like running a race. Still, he checked out and put the groceries into the truck before returning to Willy's, where he put things away and lay down on the sofa to rest, the dogs all taking places nearby.

"Uncle Kevin," Grant said as Kevin popped his eyes open, startling awake. The dogs raced excitedly to April, Willy, and Grant for attention. "Look what I made in school." He thrust a drawing forward, and Kevin took it, looking over the blobs of color, trying to see something in it. "I made a picture of you and Daddy." He was so proud, and Kevin smiled.

"It's really good," he told Grant. "Can I keep it and put it on my refrigerator at home?"

"Yes!" He punched the air and jumped like he had just won the big game. "Refrigerator. I go make more." And he was off to his room.

Kevin turned to Willy for some sort of explanation. "At school the other kids talk about having their art on the fridge. It's like an honor. And since we lost our fridge… let's just say that you made him very happy." Willy placed his hand on his shoulder. "I'm glad you were resting."

Kevin got to his feet. "I went to the store and got some things." He followed Willy into the kitchen, where he opened the fridge and gaped.

"What did you do, buy out the store?"

"I got things that you all eat. You've been feeding me for days, so I thought I should help out." He had gotten some of everything he could think of that Willy and the kids ate. He also got some special things for him and Willy.

Willy closed the door and hugged him tightly. "That was very nice. Thank you." He kissed him hard. "And maybe if you're up to it, I can say thank you properly once the kids have gone to bed."

"Daddy, can I have juice?" Grant asked.

"Yes." He got out a juice box and handed one to him and one to April, getting them both seated at the table. He got out some cheesy crackers, and the kids had a snack before going to play.

"They don't ever stop," Kevin said.

"Nope. Not until they fall asleep. April napped at daycare. They tried to get Grant to rest, but he refuses." He sat down with two mugs of coffee, one for each of them.

"How were classes?" Kevin asked, wondering about Willy's day.

"Interesting. The one class that I have is pretty typical. I'm going at the pace I usually do. The other is racing ahead of where I usually am. Their questions are so advanced." He grinned, and Kevin saw the delight in his eyes. "I love it when the concepts just click. It doesn't happen with every class, but it definitely is with this one." He sipped from his mug. "I really love what I do, but sometimes the college politics get to be too much. There are curriculum meetings and faculty committee meetings where things get discussed until all the air is sucked out of the room, yet nothing happens. They don't make a decision because they want everything to be unanimous, but it never is. I'd like to teach some newer economic theory, but I can't get the committee to agree. Most do and think it's no big deal, but one of the members was on the committee that developed the current curriculum, so he doesn't want anything to change." Willy shook his head. "So I decided to offer a seminar class in the spring that will focus on those theories. If I get enough students, then it's a no-brainer, and if I don't… then I have to keep fighting for what I want and what I think is best for the students."

"But how can you know you're right?" Kevin asked.

Willy shrugged. "The kids will tell me. If they are interested in the class, then they'll sign up because it has value for them. And if they don't, then I know that I need to look at things differently. It is economics, after all. I'll consider the seminar a win if I get ten students." He grinned. "And some of my colleagues will eat crow."

"Is one seminar going to help your students get better jobs?"

Willy shrugged. "I doubt it, but we're a liberal arts institution. Many of our students go on to other schools for postgraduate work. What we do is teach these kids to think for themselves and to reason critically. So I give them tools, and they run with them. There isn't a great deal of me standing up in front of the class talking and then giving them tests to see how much they can spew back. Their grades are based on exams, essays, and papers meant to demonstrate taking a position and defending it either by using other sources or logic." He sipped from his mug. "Before the fire, I was working on a paper, as well as the outline for a book. The paper is meant for publication in a journal, but the book is meant to explain economic principles to real people."

"Like how to understand all those numbers you hear on the news?" Kevin asked, and Willy nodded. "I hear them all the time, but they don't really mean much."

"Exactly. That's what I'm working to put together. A simple guide to what all that means. Like what does unemployment mean? Last month it was 4.1 percent. So would it surprise you if I was to say that we consider that very close to full employment? People are always leaving one job to move to another, getting fired, being hired, and so on, and at any one time, that's about 4 percent. That's what I want people to understand. But it's been hard since the fire. I try to work in my office, but I don't get a lot of time, and when I get home, the kids need me. I think I just need a chance for things to quiet down. The semester will be over in a month, and then during the summer I hope I'll be able to get drafts of both the article and my outline completed."

"You don't let anything stop you, do you?" Kevin asked.

"Not if I can help it. You're the same way." They finished their coffee, and then Willy went in to play with the kids for a while. Kevin cleaned up the kitchen and then sat on the sofa, doing his best to get comfortable as April laughed while Willy flew her around the room.

"How did you get him to go to bed so easily?" Willy asked as Kevin returned from Grant's bedroom. "He never goes to bed that easily."

Kevin sat next to Willy and put his arm around his shoulder. "I told him that Elsa was really tired but that she wasn't going to go to bed unless he did. So maybe he could go to bed so that she could." He grinned. "Worked like a charm. Elsa jumped right onto the bed and curled up next to him. Grant was so tired, he closed his eyes and was out in a few minutes. Is April asleep?"

"Yeah. She was out almost as soon as her head hit the pillow. I honestly don't know what we're going to do when you get better. Those dogs have fallen in love with the kids and vice versa. The other week, Grant kept asking me if we could go over to your house to see the dogs."

Kevin gently tilted Willy's head up to meet his gaze. "We'll figure it out." Then he kissed him, tasting those sweet lips. He wanted to press Willy back against the sofa cushions, and without even thinking, he deepened the kiss. He pulled away and turned his head before coughing.

"Hey. It's okay. You'll heal up, and then I can show you just how pleased I am that you're feeling better." His eyes danced with mischief that Kevin wished he could explore in all the best ways.

A knock sounded on the front door, and Willy got up and let Red and Carter inside. "The kids are asleep," Willy cautioned.

"How is the breathing?" Carter asked Kevin as Willy closed the door.

"I'm improving. I wish it was faster."

Carter nodded. "I think we had some luck. I was able to take the drawing we came up with, and I compared it to the DMV database. That search came up with a local man." He showed them the image from his license photo.

"That's him," Willy said right away. "That's the man who came here twice."

Kevin nodded. "Yeah. That's the guy I scared off. Will you bring him in for questioning?" He really wanted to get behind what was going on.

"More likely we'll go to his house to find out what he was doing here. We'll get to the bottom of this." Red sounded so sure, it made Kevin feel more confident. "Have you seen him since?"

"Nothing other than a stupid note. There hasn't been anyone hanging around that we've seen," Kevin said, meeting Willy's gaze before he nodded. "It's been quiet, which makes me wonder what this guy is up to. He isn't really very good at threatening people, and you'd think…."

"What?"

"That a business with connections like Kraft and Hobson would do a better job of it. Not that I want people harassing Willy and the kids, but this guy seems very amateur." Kevin couldn't quite put his finger on it, but something was off.

"I feel the same way. I easily got the drop on him."

Red made notes. "Okay, we'll find out what's going on."

"Can you let us know?" Willy asked.

Carter hesitated, but Red answered. "We will if we can. With an ongoing investigation, there are limits to what we can say. But we will tell you if we can."

"I can't ask for more than that," Willy said. "Is there anything more that we can do to help you? I have coffee if you'd like some."

"No, we're all right. Carter and I wanted to make sure that we had the right person," Red explained. "Thank you both for your time. We'll see ourselves out."

"Thank you," Willy said as they left. "This is so confusing to me." He sat down again, and Kevin drew him close. "What I really wish is to understand what is going on and why I was burned out of my home. Why we needed to move." He lowered his head slowly. "I wish this had never happened."

Kevin swallowed. "But what if you had never met me?" He didn't mean to blurt that out, but the sudden hurt that went through him wouldn't be stopped.

Willy lightly stroked his cheek. "You have been the best thing to come out of this, and I don't regret anything about that. Maybe it's true that when a door closes, a window opens… and you are the best, biggest, sexiest window I have ever seen." He wrapped his arms around Kevin's waist. "I want my life back. I know we have a better place for the kids and everything, but it still feels like I'm… I don't know… living someone else's life? Like I'm a guest in my own mind."

"I think that's probably natural. You've had a lot of change. But the kids are happy, they are safe… and so are you." He squeezed a little tighter. "Nothing is going to happen."

Willy sniffed. "I know. But I keep having these dreams that the house is on fire and I can't get to the kids. They are blocked off by a wall of fire, and all I can do is call for them until someone drags me out, and I have to watch the house fall in around them." He shook, and Kevin held him tighter, rocking gently.

"It's okay. The kids are in their rooms sleeping, and you were the one who kept your head and got the kids almost out of the building. They survived because of you. So remember that."

"But the dreams seem so real. I know they aren't, but I wake up terrified whenever I have one, and I have to remind myself that it isn't real and that I'm safe. I'm petrified that it's going to happen again."

"And we've done everything we can to make sure it doesn't," Kevin said. "Do you think you should find someone to speak to? We have people we work with at the department. They help a lot."

"I'll think about it." Kevin supposed that was about the best answer he could get at the moment. "I really will."

"Hey. It was a suggestion. I know we've talked, but maybe talking to someone else could help. I know you're worried and that some of that is wrapped up with me because of what I do."

Willy nodded. "Everything is this big, giant ball of worry that sits in my gut. I keep hoping it will go away, but it just sits there. I know some of it is just because everything happened so fast. The fire, the new apartment, this asshole threatening us, and the fact that all of it may be caused by someone wanting to burn down my building…." He shivered. "I keep wondering what if they come after me? What's to stop them from burning down this place? Or my building at the college?"

Damn, Kevin hadn't realized things had gotten so bad for Willy. He had thought that over time, it would get easier, but things seemed to have become worse, with Willy's active imagination working overtime. Kevin wished he could do something to help him, but had no idea what. He was a man of action. When someone needed something, his first instinct was to jump in and get things done. This was not one of those times. There was nothing he could do except be there for him.

He thought he would give it a try. "You aren't actively investigating the fire or asking questions. You've been busy getting your life together, and that's your job. I've been investigating, and right now, we don't have much to go on. But there is nothing to bring their attention to you. We're going to get to the bottom of these threats damned soon. Carter and Red will see to that, and there hasn't been anyone watching the house in a while."

"Not that we've seen, anyway."

"True. But I really think we scared this guy away. Something about him doesn't make sense, but we'll figure it out."

Willy sighed. "I know I'm being stupid. That I'm letting my mind run away with me. I've had you here for days, my own personal fireman." He patted Kevin's chest. "Do you know what I want right now, more than anything? I want you to help me forget about all this… if only for a little while."

"Okay. I think I can do that," he whispered. "Go to your room and get undressed. I'll be right in." Kevin waited for Willy to get up before quietly going into the bathroom. There was a medicine cabinet, and Kevin checked inside and found what he wanted. Then he joined Willy in the bedroom, closing the door. He turned out the lights and partially parted the curtains to the backyard, letting in some of the ambient light.

"What are you doing?" Willy asked, his pale skin almost glowing.

Kevin spread a large towel on the bed and guided Willy onto it. "Just relax." He toed off his shoes and then slipped out of his pants and T-shirt before slowly climbing on the bed.

"You know you can't do too much…."

"It's okay," Kevin whispered before putting some lotion on his hands and then lightly touching Willy's shoulders. At first Willy shivered, but as Kevin stroked over his shoulders and back, the heat between his hands and Willy's skin warmed them both. "Take deep breaths, let go of the tension, and just let yourself enjoy it." He made a long stroke down Willy's back and then up to his shoulders, earning a soft groan that warmed Kevin's heart and made him want things he knew he couldn't have, at least for now.

CHAPTER 13

KEVIN HAD magic hands; that was all there was to it. Willy lay stretched out on the bed as Kevin worked the backs of his legs. Willy wanted to ask him where he learned to do this, but the fact was that he didn't have the energy, and he certainly didn't want to break the moment between them. He worried that he had sounded really whiny earlier, and he wished he could take back everything he'd said. But at the moment, with Kevin's glorious hands working the back of his leg and down his calf to his foot, he found himself gasping as tension released from his muscles.

"Sweetheart, you've been holding tension all over." Kevin continued the massage, moving to Willy's other leg. "And you need to release it." He continued working down his leg and then his foot, sending a tingling sensation up Willy's back. Willy lay still as more and more tension left him. For the first time in weeks, he didn't feel as though he were being tied in knots. They were coming undone, and the pressure and worry flowed out of him. He had no idea how long this would last, but it felt damn good.

"That's it," Kevin whispered as he made long strokes up his legs and back before descending again, all the way to his feet. "Let's roll over."

"Okay," Willy whispered and turned over. Kevin shifted to his shoulders and neck, working more tension out of them. "How…?"

"I took classes in massage therapy a few years ago. The guys at the station are always complaining about aches and tension. But once I finished the classes, I realized how uncomfortable it was to work on the guys, so my skills didn't go anywhere… until now. I'm a little rusty, but…."

Willy released a deep breath and closed his eyes. He found he didn't have the energy to talk, so he just let go of everything and lay quietly, letting Kevin's incredible hands work their magic. Breathing deeply, he kept his eyes closed, concentrating only on where Kevin touched him.

After a few minutes, he opened his eyes and found himself looking into Kevin's. He didn't move as he drew closer, hands pausing on his chest. "You are so beautiful like this." He drew even closer and then kissed him. Willy arched his back and returned the kiss, which quickly grew heated.

"We can't do this," Willy whispered as warmth and desire flooded through him. He had been holding himself at bay for days, and his control was definitely beginning to wane.

"Like I said, sweetheart, there are ways…." Kevin's voice grew rough, and as he kissed Willy, his slick hand slid down his belly before his fingers closed around Willy's cock.

Willy closed his eyes, letting the sensation wash over him. "Kevin," he moaned softly before kissing him hard, bringing his arms up to hold him. He arched his back, shaking as the desire he'd held back came charging forward. "You don't need to do this."

"I do. I want you to know what I feel for you and that I care. You need to relax and let go of all the tension." Kevin stroked harder, his fingers lightly bumping along the edge of his cockhead, driving Willy out of his mind. It wasn't long before his entire body felt like it was on fire. His breathing grew ragged, and he gasped, his mouth hanging open.

He held himself under control for as long as he could, hanging on to Kevin for fear he was going to fly apart. Then, as Kevin drew him to the edge, he stilled and held his breath as Kevin stroked him harder, slowing the speed but increasing the pressure until Willy could take it no longer and tumbled over the precipice of passion, gasping as he tried not to cry out, even though he wanted to scream his release from the roof.

Wrung out, Willy lay still on the bed, breathing deeply, too exhausted to think. "What did you do to me?" he asked and then smiled as Kevin kissed him lightly and then turned away, coughing from deep in his lungs. "What did you do?"

Kevin cleared his throat. "I couldn't help myself. Things got a little out of hand…." He coughed again, this time less deeply, and Willy rolled onto his side to look at him. "It was worth it… so worth it."

"You need to be more careful," Willy told him before shifting off the towel and using it to wipe himself up. "I think that maybe we should shower before coming back to bed." He was most definitely a mess, and he figured Kevin could use a wash as well. "We have to be quiet. So…."

"I don't have the energy for a second round anyway."

He took Kevin's hand and led him to the bathroom. After starting the shower, he let the water warm and got under the spray. Kevin joined him, and Willy let the water sluice over both of them before pressing

Kevin back and taking the soap from the dish. Now it was his turn to show Kevin how he felt.

WILLY SLEPT like a log and woke remembering no dreams at all, which was a relief. He was still relaxed as he rolled over and Kevin slipped his arms around him, spooning him. "The kids are still asleep, and there's no need to get up yet."

"I have a class at nine," Willy said quietly and closed his eyes again. After all, who was he to slough off a few more minutes of quiet?

A soft knock and then jumping outside the door caught his attention. That could only mean one thing: April. He got out of bed and pulled on his robe before opening the door to his daughter and Benjamin standing in the hallway. "We hungry," she said.

"Okay." He took her hand and led her to her room, where he got her out of her nighttime Pull-Ups and then had her go potty before he dressed her. "Go play with your dolly, and I'll get dressed and make you breakfast." He had slept well but was still tired. "Where's Grant?"

He peered in his son's room and found him on the floor in his pajamas, playing with trucks. "Bekfas," April said, and Grant raced out of the room, Elsa right behind him.

"Grant, go get dressed. I set out your clothes last night. Then you can come down to eat. Can you do that?"

"I can, I'm big." He hurried back to his room, and Willy took a few minutes to dress before getting both kids to the kitchen, where he put some french toast sticks in the toaster. He also got out juice and made up plates for both of them.

Kevin joined them as he got the kids' food and poured himself a mug of coffee. "Red just called. He says he needs to meet with us."

"Can they come to my office at ten thirty? I have to get the kids to daycare, and I need to get to my class. I can't be late." Willy checked the time once more before making up the kids' lunches and their school bags. Then he got them ready to go.

"They said they'll meet us at your office," Kevin followed up. They shared a kiss, and then Willy was off, hoping he could get the kids checked in quickly and get to his office with enough time to get the materials he had prepared.

Of course there was a line at drop-off, but he got both kids checked in and then raced to the college, grateful he found a parking spot quickly. He hurried to his office, grabbed his materials, and got to his classroom with five minutes to spare.

This was one of his favorite classes, and the students were always so energized. They asked a great many questions, and the class flew by. By the time he finished answering their questions after the lesson, he was nearly late.

"The police are outside your office with my nephew," Evelyn told him as he entered the building. She must have been waiting for him. "What's going on?"

"At this point I don't know exactly, and I don't have time to bring you up to date, but no one is in trouble… except the people who are." God, that sounded weird even to him. "Kevin is fine. So am I and the kids."

She narrowed her gaze. "You better let me know."

He steeled his own in return. "You know the rule. No gossip."

She snickered and rolled her eyes. "It's too late for that. The police will have set everyone's tongues wagging."

"Then I'll give them something to gossip about." He turned and climbed the stairs, swishing his backside to and fro. From her laughter, he knew Evelyn got the message.

Willy turned the corner on the second floor and found Kevin and the two officers. He stopped as he recognized the fourth person in their group. "You better have a good explanation for this," he growled, "or else this guy is going to be huddling on the ground with his nuts in his hands… again."

Red stepped forward. "We wouldn't have brought him here if we didn't think you needed to hear what he has to say. Is there a place we can speak privately?" Willy's office was too small.

Kevin hurried over to him.

"There's a faculty break room. We can go there." He led the way, opening the door to the empty room. They went inside, and Willy sat at one of the tables, thankful that Kevin took the seat next to him. "Okay. Why are we here?"

"Like Red said, we wouldn't do this if we didn't feel it was necessary." Red and Carter sat on either side of the man who had threatened Willy and Kevin.

"I didn't intend to cause you any harm."

"Then why make fucking threats?" Willy growled. "You scared me half to death, and I have kids. Do you know I spent every night for the last ten days looking out my windows, watching to see if I was followed? And all of that is because of you, so whatever you think you were doing, you really don't know shit." He stood. "Are we done here? I have important things that I need to do, and listening to a bunch of crap is a waste of my time. I will press charges for his threats, and I'll talk to a lawyer about a restraining order if I have to." He was ready to leave.

"I got burned out of my home the same way you did," the man said. "I lived in an apartment on the edge of Middletown. I got burned out because Kraft and Hobson did a shit job of building the place. No one did a damned thing about it. So when I heard that someone was investigating them, I thought if I applied a little pressure then people would be less likely to give up."

"What the hell?" Willy asked in disbelief. "You threatened me because you thought that Kevin and I had some authority and that we'd just give up? That's kind of fucked up. You could have just knocked on the door and said, 'Hey, I'm Joe Blow and the same thing happened to me.' That would have been a lot more helpful." He shook his head.

"We checked out his story," Carter said. "That's why we're here with him. We believe what he's telling us. His methods were a little messed up, but he did live in a building that burned, and it was built by the same people who built yours."

"I think they torched it because people were starting to sniff around. They were using substandard materials and cut a ton of corners. The residents began having a lot of issues, so we were looking into things, and suddenly the building goes up in flames one night. Everyone got out, but some kids were hurt because of it. Everyone in the building lost everything, and while the fire department investigated—they even called it arson—things petered out and no one was charged. Now it looks like they've done the same thing here. More than once."

Red and Carter both nodded. "It looks that way. But we don't have any records, and there isn't much left of either building for us to investigate. They managed to make sure whatever evidence there might be is pretty much ashes or a tangled mess."

Kevin cleared his throat. "We have looked at what we can, but like you said, there's very little left. As best we can put together, they simply spread gasoline on the remaining framework, and it went up hot and fast."

"Check the concrete."

"Excuse me?" Kevin asked.

"One of the ways they cheat is substandard concrete, so check the foundations. Those didn't burn, and you may be able to find a pattern there. No one checked that on my building, but I talked to some of the demo crew who cleared away what remained, and they were remarking about how easy it was and that the job didn't take very long. I take that to mean that the concrete was easy to dismantle and probably not up to code."

Red and Carter made notes. "I can have that done," Red said. "We can also check that against the specs that the borough has." He turned to the man they had brought. "And no making threats to anyone. That isn't the way to get attention. If you had come to us, things would have been a lot easier. As it is, any information you give us has to be treated skeptically because of your behavior, and that means more work for us. And if we are able to build a case, we can't ask you to testify because of the attempted intimidation."

"I understand. But you have to realize that these people have their minions everywhere, and when they don't, they buy them. It's that simple." He sounded desperate.

"What did you lose in the fire?" Willy asked, calming down somewhat. He tried to think about what he would do to get to the bottom of all this, and a little harassment wasn't out of the realm of possibility if he thought it might get results. Though he hoped he would do a better job of it and track down the people who truly deserved to stay awake at night.

"Everything. All the family pictures, the things I got from my grandparents. Yeah, I got out, but ever since then I've felt like…."

"Like part of your past and who you are has been ripped away?" Willy supplied, his anger evaporating when he got a nod.

"I've been so lost. I find myself looking for something and then remembering that it's gone. I know it's only stuff, but there are memories attached to those things—or there were—and it's like losing those memories too."

Willy could understand that. "The same thing happened to me. But my situation was made worse because I was threatened." He leaned against Kevin, letting him be his strength for a little while. He felt wiped out, but at least he had an answer for part of what was going on. "I'm Willy, by the way." He realized he didn't know the man's name.

"Frankie White," the other man said. "I know I handled this badly and I shouldn't have shown up at your house, but I needed help and didn't know if I'd get it. No one else seemed to understand." This man was definitely lost, and Willy hoped like hell that he never got to that point.

"We are going to get to the bottom of this. Don't worry about that. And I'm not going to press charges, but get the help you need. Talk to someone who can help you deal with this." Willy had heard of people losing themselves in a cycle of grief and loss and not being able to get out. He'd just never met anyone like that before. But then, losing your home was traumatic. That kind of shakeup could be tough, and Willy had the idea that Frankie was alone. At least Willy had plenty of support—Kevin, Ellen, Evelyn, and other people who filled his life. Going through this alone would be frightening as all hell. "I bet Red and Carter can help you with that. They're good officers."

Carter seemed taken by surprise. "So everything is okay?"

Willy shrugged. "We have an explanation, and that's good enough for now." It lifted the threat of intimidation and someone watching the house. But someone still needed to pay for the destruction of his home—and everyone else's. "Do you need to take Frankie home?"

"He came here to talk to you of his own volition, so Mr. White is free to go," Red said, and Frankie looked around and then stood. He left the room but stopped at the door.

"I wish I had had people like you after the fire." He looked almost broken as he left.

Willy was tempted to go after him, and maybe he should have, but he stayed in his chair. There was nothing he could do for Frankie. If Frankie wanted to change his life, then he needed to do it himself.

"I'll get the concrete tested," Carter said.

"That will help," Kevin added.

Willy shook his head. "No, it won't. We already know that they cut corners. There's plenty of evidence, and if we wanted to go after Kraft and Hobson, we could do that now. But what good is it going to do? This was years ago, and they'll blame it on former management and go right on. There's no proof to tie them to any of the fires."

Red put his hands on the table. "What do you propose to do? Not give up, I hope."

"God, no. They have ruined a lot of people's lives, and they need to pay. If they keep it up, they are going to kill someone." He tapped his fingers on top of the table. "Can you find out every building they built in this area? There have to be more." An idea was taking shape in his mind.

"What are you thinking?" Carter asked.

"Well, we need to find out what they worked on, then see if there is a building we can use as bait. Let it be known that we are investigating this particular building for code violations and quite possibly criminal fraud. You can put together the proper language to make it sound really official and that the department here is serious about taking them down. If they burned what was left of my building, as well as others, to cover up what they are doing, then our threat will have to be neutralized."

Kevin gasped. "But that means putting others in danger. as well as other property."

Willy nodded. "I know. And that's why we need to find out everything they worked on. I don't know if there is a building that we could use as bait. Understand, I don't want more people put in danger, but as long as these criminals are in business, everyone living in any of those buildings is threatened if every time someone suspects what they are doing, they torch the evidence. Someone is going to get hurt."

Red leaned forward. "I can see if I can get that information, but we're going to have to proceed carefully."

"I know. And I'm not saying that it's something we can do, but we have to look into setting a trap for them. I think it may be the only way to bring all of this to an end. All we need is to get a couple of their people, and from there you should be able to go up the line. At least it would be a place to start."

"Okay. We'll look into it. But I'm not making any promises," Red told them.

Willy rolled his eyes. "I'm not asking you to commit to anything. But a trap, coordinated between the police and fire departments, could be a way to flush these people out. They don't waste time, so it wouldn't be a long operation. It would be a matter of finding a property where no one could get hurt." He could see it now and leaned over the table. "These people do a crap job installing the fire-suppression systems. So make sure it's working in the building you intend to use as a trap. That way whatever they do isn't going to get very far."

Carter nodded and smiled. "I get it. They are going to count on their shoddy work helping them."

"Exactly. Make sure the system is working, so that if there is a fire, the system kicks in and douses it in the area affected without damaging the rest of the building. In the meantime, the fire department is on alert because they know what's happening, and the police department can have the building under surveillance so that they catch the people intent on setting the fire. If we're lucky, you catch them before they actually set the fire." The more he thought about it, the more he knew it could work. "Or is this too much like a television episode?"

Carter and Red spoke softly. "We'll look into the idea, but under no circumstances is either of you to take it upon yourselves to get involved. We don't want you two on their radar. Is that understood?"

Willy nodded. "I just wanted to share my idea. I'm a father of two, and I'm not going to put myself or my kids in danger." And the thought of Kevin being on the front line scared him too. "As long as we promise not to go out on our own, do you promise to keep me informed?"

They looked at each other. "I'm not sure we can comment on an ongoing investigation."

Willy put his hands on his hips. "Then there is nothing to stop me from heading down to Borough Hall and asking the codes department for all the building projects that Kraft and Hobson worked on. They are public records, and I can use the Freedom of Information Act to get whatever I need, especially if it's part of my work. I've decided that an economic impact study of certain classes of buildings might yield some interesting results. After all, I'm always looking for another chance to publish."

Carter looked about ready to blow his top, but Red rolled his eyes. "Fine. We'll keep you informed as much as we can, as long as you stay away from the case yourself. There is no need to put yourself on the front line. Got it."

"Agreed." Willy checked the time. "Classes are about to let out, which means half the faculty will be in here, and all of them are going to want to know what you wanted. So unless you want to face a dozen academics whose natural inclination is to ask questions, you might want to say goodbye. The rumor mill here works faster than at a garden club tea."

Red snickered. "Thanks. We'll be in touch." They left the room.

A few minutes later classes ended, and Willy sighed. "That was close."

"How so?"

"The only person who saw them come in was your aunt, and I can trust her to keep her mouth shut. But if the rest of these gossips saw us with the police, the rumors would fly around this place, and I can imagine they would range from me being mugged to I'm wanted for murder. God only knows." There were times when he thought the people he worked with needed to get lives of their own.

"I'll head out. You need to get ready for your next class." Kevin stood and lightly kissed him before leaving the break room.

"Jesus, the good ones are either married or gay," Violet, an ancient history professor, said from behind him. "What I wouldn't give," she added, watching Kevin.

"He's my nephew," Evelyn snapped. She and Violet never got along. "And he has good taste." She patted Willy's cheek. "What was all that about?"

"Nothing. Just an update on what they're doing about the fire." That should keep the rumor mill at bay. "They're making progress, but they don't have a lot of definitive answers yet. In other words, they know some things but can't share them. Which is fine. The kids and I are safe, and Kevin is doing better. That's what counts."

"So he's going back to work soon?"

"Hopefully in a few days. The cough is getting better, but it hasn't gone away." He was starting to get worried that Kevin's lungs were injured more than they thought. "I'm keeping an eye on him as much as he will allow me."

She rolled her eyes. "That one is a really good man, but he spends all his time worrying about other people and doesn't take good enough care of himself. If he'd had his own way, he would have returned to work the next day and pretended everything was all right until he keeled over from sheer exhaustion and lack of oxygen." She poured herself some coffee. "You're good for him."

"I'm not so sure about that. I come with a lot of baggage, so to speak. And I hope it doesn't prove to be too much. The kids love him…."

"And that's got you scared, because if he leaves, then the kids will be affected."

Willy nodded. "I could get so attached to having him in our lives. But can I do that? Can I take that chance? It's not just me, and the longer he's around, the more they'll…." He knew she understood. "I just don't want them to get hurt. I can deal with myself, but not what I'm opening them up to."

Evelyn shook her head. "People are going to come and go from your kids' lives all the time. The only person who isn't going to do that is you. So stop worrying. Those kids are going to grow to love the same people you do, particularly at this age. If you want a relationship, then have one. If you don't, then Kevin deserves to know how you feel and what you're thinking."

Willy sighed. "That's just it—I don't know. I mean, I know how I feel, but what if I don't feel the same in the future, or what if Kevin decides it's all too much?"

Evelyn sipped from her mug. "It sounds like you want guarantees, and there aren't any. We're all flying blind every time we give our heart. Mark's death really did a number on you."

"Well, I thought that was going to last forever, and look what happened there. I thought we would be together forever, but I didn't know that only meant…." He hadn't thought of Mark in a while, and maybe that was part of what was bothering him.

"Mark was wonderful, I know that, but don't let your fears keep you from having a second chance."

He nodded. "I mean, after Mark, I never thought I'd feel that way again and…." He wanted to get the hell out of this room because his feelings were way too close to the surface. "I guess I'm worried that I might be forgetting about him."

"It's just that the loss you've carried along with you for so long is starting to fade. That's healthy. It means that you're ready to move on. Mark will always be in your heart, and so will your kids."

"But…."

"Did your love for Grant diminish when you had April?" she asked. "Of course not. Your heart just expanded to include them both. And that's what's happening. Making room for someone new doesn't mean that you let go. Mark is part of your past, and you loved him. Maybe Kevin is part of your future."

"I hope he is."

"Then maybe it's as simple as you allowing him to be," Evelyn offered. "Now you go on and get to your next class and don't worry so much about what's best for everyone else. Think about what's going to make you happy." She flashed him a smile, and Willy went to his office to get his materials. Damn, he was messed up, and he needed to get his head on straight. He didn't want to screw things up with Kevin, but losing Mark had left him with so much fear and worry.

He was being dumb, and he knew it. Kevin was a good person, and he wasn't going to hurt Willy, at least not on purpose. And the future hadn't happened yet, so worrying about it was kind of dumb. It was time he allowed himself to start living again, and that meant going on with his life, moving forward. He took a deep breath and smiled to himself before heading off to his next class.

WILLY WAS never so happy that a day was over in his life. He was sick of answering the same question about why the police were there. Even the damned dean had taken him aside to ask what was going on.

"Do I need to send out an email to the entire department explaining why they were here and that everyone needs to get their nose out of my business, or should I just send that to you?" he had snapped before leaving his office.

"I'm just concerned," the dean had said.

Willy turned around. "The time to be concerned was when my home burned to the ground and I lost everything, but no one seemed to give a damn then, so I suggest you all butt out now." He continued down the hall under a full head of steam, pissed as hell and getting angrier by the second. He knew he should have kept quiet, but he was tired of the gossip and nosiness.

When he returned to his office, he found two students waiting for him. "Can I help you?" He tried to remember that these were the people he was here for and forced himself to calm down.

The young man and woman each carried books. He knew Jane and Roger from his second-year economics class. "Was the man who left right after the police your boyfriend?" Jane asked. "There was a rumor that you were seeing someone."

Willy hesitated.

"I just wanted to say 'way to go,' if he was."

Willy found himself laughing. There were no secrets in this place, and there never would be. Expecting anything else was a pipe dream. "Yes. He and I have been seeing each other."

"Cool. You deserve someone nice," she said. "Have a good night." The two of them went down the hall, and Willy wondered why his social life was so fascinating to so many people.

He headed out to the parking lot and was about to get in his car when the dean came out of the building. Willy thought about getting in his car and driving away, pretending he hadn't seen him, but before he could, the dean said, "Willy, you were correct."

"And I apologize for being snappy. I asked the officers to meet me at my office because it was the only time I had today. I should have found time to meet them at my house, but they said it was important." In the future he would keep anything personal as far away from the college as possible.

"Is everything all right? Do you or your family need anything?" the dean asked.

"No. The kids and I are doing our best to rebuild our lives. It's taking time, but we're managing. Evelyn helped make sure the kids had some of the things they needed." Willy wasn't sure what the dean wanted or if this was a show of contrition. "It's just taking time to put our lives back together."

"Are there financial issues at this point?"

"Some, but the insurance company has approved my claim. They said it will take a few more days for the payment to process. Once that happens, then everything should loosen up. But thank you for asking."

He nodded. "Don't hesitate to let me know if there is anything the department or the college can to do to help."

"Thank you." Willy regretted being sharp with him. It wasn't the dean's fault. He was busy trying to keep all of the academic wheels in motion, and that was one heck of a task. "I appreciate that." He got into his car and drove to the daycare, where he went to April's room first.

"How was school?" he asked April, who seemed subdued.

The teacher hurried over. "She had a little accident today. We got her cleaned up and everything." There was always an extra outfit in her school bag just in case. "She's been upset about it."

"I a big girl," she said softly as Willy picked her up.

"You're daddy's big girl, and things like that happen."

"They call me Stinky," April moaned before burying her head against Willy's shoulder. He patted her back and thanked the teacher before carrying her down to Grant's room. He was ready and excited to get home, talking the entire time to the car and then on the drive home.

His chatter continued into the house but stopped abruptly. "He's asleep," Grant stage-whispered.

"Not for long if you keep talking like that." Willy took Grant's hand and led him into the kitchen, carrying April, who was still quiet. He got them both a snack, and April finally began to open up as they ate.

A few minutes later, Kevin came in. "You're home?" He stretched, his shirt riding up to show some of his belly. Willy couldn't resist running his fingers along the exposed skin.

"Yeah. It was a weird day, as you can imagine. Everyone asked me about why the police were at my office. I should have thought more about that meeting. Next time they can come here. At least I won't have half the faculty and students wondering if I'm in trouble." He shook his head. "How about you? How are you feeling?"

"A lot better. I haven't been coughing much at all. I spoke to the chief, and we agreed that I should return in a week. So that's pretty good."

Willy nodded. "Ummm. Have you given any thought to when you'd go back to your house?" He hadn't wanted to ask the question because he didn't want Kevin to think that he wanted him to leave. It was comfortable having Kevin here with them, and he didn't want to push him out—more like he wanted a chance to prepare himself for being alone again.

CHAPTER 14

KEVIN HAD sidestepped Willy's question because he hadn't seen it coming and because he wondered if Willy was getting tired of him, but he couldn't keep his questions to himself forever.

"What is it you want?" Kevin asked Willy that night after the kids were asleep.

"Me? What about you?" Willy asked.

"Are you getting tired of me? Do you want me to go? I can. I mean, I'm doing fine, and I'll be back to work soon."

It was Willy's turn to cough. "No, I'm not tired of you. And for whatever reason, you fit with this little family. The kids think the world of you, and I…." He left another of those Willy pauses that made Kevin wonder what he was really thinking. "Are we going too fast? A few days ago we were talking about taking things slow, and now we've spent the majority of the time we've known each other living together and even sleeping together. I don't think this is the way things are supposed to work." Sometimes Willy was so conventionally cute.

"I get that. I really do. But it's how things seemed to work out. You stepped in to help me when I needed you."

"And you did the same for me when you barely knew me and the kids. But I guess I need to know where things go from here. You're feeling better, and I guess I figured you would be ready to go back to your own life—or something that resembled what you had before we came crashing through it."

Kevin rolled his eyes. "Do you know what I had before I met you? Work—and more work. I didn't have a life, not really. You saw my house. It was largely empty because I was never there. I worked a lot and was always the guy willing to take an extra shift because someone needed it. Now I have you and the kids and a chance at a life I thought was only for other people. I figured I'd go home tomorrow because I have to get used to being on my own again."

Willy snickered. "That's why I was asking—so I could get used to being on my own again."

Kevin shook his head. "Then we can play it by ear. There aren't any rules about how things are supposed to work. It's just you and me and how we want to go forward." He paused as the front door jangled. He continued listening and then went to the old mail slot next to the door. A piece of paper had been pushed through, and Kevin picked it up by a corner.

Back Off or Else! Anyone Can Get Burned! was written in black block letters like the other note.

"What is it?" Willy asked as he came in. Then he saw the note. "What the heck is going on? Do you think Frankie did this?"

"No. This is different, and I think it's directed at me." Kevin set down the page before picking up the phone to call Carter. "Maybe the first one was too."

Carter answered with, "What's up?"

"We received another threatening note. I thought the first one was sent by Frankie, but I don't think he would be dumb enough to leave a note after our conversation today."

"Do you have both of them?" Carter asked.

"I have the one we just received. Unfortunately Benjamin got hold of the first one and decided it was a chew toy. I only touched the corner of this one. Do you or Red want to stop by and get it?" Kevin was getting really angry. Just when one thing seemed settled, another popped up.

"How is Willy taking it?"

"That's the thing. I think this one is aimed at me, which means that I've been followed." He wasn't sure what he thought about that. "And it means that because I've been staying with Willy since my accident, I've brought this mess to his door. We have to get to the bottom of it fast."

"I'll come by first thing in the morning to get the note. You keep all the doors and windows locked. I'm going to put out a note for the night patrols to make their presence known in your area. If someone is watching, that will give them pause."

"I hope so."

Carter told Kevin to stay alert, and they ended the call. There was nothing more he could do. Kevin thought about going home right now, but that would only leave Willy and the kids alone in the house. It was safer with all of them together.

He checked all the windows and doors, making sure everything was locked, including the gate to the yard. Then he explained what Carter had said to Willy.

"It's okay. We have this."

"Yeah, we do. I'll stay out here tonight, and you go on to bed."

"No." Willy took his hand. "Come on. It's late and we're both tired. And I want a night with you." He led Kevin to his room and closed the door.

"Do you think this is a good idea?" Kevin asked softly.

Willy let go of his hand and turned to him. "Nothing is going to happen to any of us as long as you're here."

"How do you know that?"

"Because you will move heaven and earth to make sure we're all safe. Well, I think it's time that someone looked after you the same way you watch over all of us. So tonight, after I rock your world, we'll keep the door open and listen." Willy drew closer. "I think it's time we figure this shit out, and then we can get our heads around what's happening between us."

"Okay. If that's what you think best."

Willy shrugged. "I don't know crap about what's best. Hell, I don't think I know about anything right now. My life is about as twisted as it gets, but there are some things I'm coming to understand, and one of them is that I can count on you. But I don't want to be a burden or someone that you think you need to protect because it's in your DNA or something."

Kevin pulled him into his arms. "I would never do that. Helping people is part of who I am, but that doesn't extend to taking them to bed or watching out for them or their kids. Those things I do because of you, so stop worrying. I love April and Grant. They're special."

"That they are. But, well… you just wait until my mother and father come to visit. I suspect you'll reevaluate your feelings then."

Kevin tugged him nearer. "Okay. First thing, we are in your bedroom with the door closed. I have my arms around you, and I'm thinking of all the delicious ways to get you out of your clothes… and you're talking about your mother."

Willy couldn't help groaning. "She sent me an email. Apparently she's worried about the kids and the fire, so she's coming out for a visit to make sure that her grandchildren are living in a proper environment."

"What?"

"She has very definite ideas on parenting, especially mine. She loved Mark, and everything was fine until he passed away. Then she got it into her head that the kids shouldn't be raised by a single parent. Let's just say that I do my best to keep her visits short at the moment."

"Did she try to take the kids?" He could feel his anger rising.

"No. But she can be a little overbearing, like she knows best. She was quiet right after the fire, but I think she's making up for lost time."

"Then let her come. You're a great father, and you put those kids above everything else. As it should be." Kevin slipped his hands under Willy's shirt, found a nipple, and gave it a light tweak. Willy hissed softly. "That's a father's job. My job is to make sure you remember that you are a man and sexy as hell, in addition to being a father."

"But my mother can—"

"Stay in her box for now. Along with threats, stupid messages, and everything else. Right now it's you and me, and the rest of the world can go to hell for a few hours. Okay?"

Willy moaned softly as Kevin tugged off his shirt and sucked on his smooth, soft skin. "Are you trying to make me crazy?"

"If you can still talk, then I'm not doing a very good job." He captured Willy's lips and kissed him until he was breathless and shaking in his arms. At least that should keep him quiet for a while. Kevin had already learned that the best way to stop Willy from worrying was to blow his mind in the best way possible, and it looked like he had just succeeded.

"Daddy!" The cry broke through everything. Willy tumbled to the floor in his haste to get to his son, and Kevin helped him up as Grant cried out again. Willy grabbed his shirt off the floor and raced out of the room like the hounds of hell were after him.

"What's wrong?" Willy asked as soon as he got into the room, picking up Grant. Kevin was right behind him.

"Fire, lots of fire," Grant said through tears. "Right there." He pointed toward the bedroom window.

Kevin left the room and hurried out the front door to the side of the building between them and the neighbors. The street was quiet, and he covered his mouth as he coughed before looking over the area under Grant's window. He didn't see anything, and he doubted he would. Nothing had been burned, and there were no signs of footprints as far as he could tell. It was likely just a nightmare. Out of caution, he checked the rest of the outside before returning inside and locking the door.

"I didn't see anything outside," he told Willy, who was still holding Grant, rocking him slowly. "What about April?"

Willy sighed. "She will sleep through a tornado, thank God," he said as Grant quieted.

"Daddy, I wanna sleep wiff you," Grant whispered.

Willy looked at Kevin, who nodded, because what else was he supposed to do? His plans for making sounds of a very different variety were going up in smoke, or more accurately with the fear of a four-year-old.

"Okay, but you gotta stop crying. I'm here, and nothing is going to hurt you." Willy carried Grant to the master bedroom and got him under the covers. Then he took off his shirt and pants, slipped into bed, and turned out the light. Kevin got out of his shirt and pants and got under the covers next to Willy.

"I love you, Daddy," Grant said softly into the darkness.

"I love you too. Now go to sleep. You have to go to school in the morning." Thankfully Grant hushed, but Elsa and Thumper took places at the foot of the bed. Jesus, this bed was as full as it was going to get. Kevin could only hope that April and Benjamin didn't end up in here with them. The poor bed frame would probably collapse, and they'd all end up sleeping on the floor.

"If fire comes, will Uncle Kevin save us?" Grant asked a few minutes later.

"There isn't going to be any more fire. And yes, Uncle Kevin will save us. Now go to sleep or you'll have to go back to your own bed. It's late, and we all need to get some rest." Willy was so patient, and thankfully that was the last they heard from Grant that night, but the dogs were another matter. Every time Kevin moved his legs, he got a growl from either Elsa or Thumper until he finally found a comfortable spot and settled to sleep.

KEVIN WAITED for Carter to pick up the note before getting his things together. Moving home was about as exciting as a toothache. The dogs went inside and checked their bowls, wandered through the house to make sure everything was still in place, and then sat watching him, like they were wondering where the kids were. Their toys were left unplayed with, and even the things hidden under the sofa were ignored.

"I know, guys, it seems strange." He went upstairs to his bedroom and put away his things and took the dirty clothes to the washer in the basement. Once all those chores were done, he ended up watching television to pass the time.

His phone rang after noon, and Kevin snatched it up, completely bored. "What's going on?"

"We got something," Chase told him. "I was working with Red and Carter to see what we could find in the rubble of the apartment building, and it's a miracle that place was standing at all. The foundation concrete was substandard and is crumbling in places. They sent it off for testing, but there is no way it should behave like that, even after a fire. Accelerant was definitely used, and we tested for residue."

"So once the tests come back, we have a case against them?"

"Red and Carter aren't so sure. Maybe not a legal case, but definitely a public safety one. They said that they will prepare a media statement. At least that should get people's attention and bring the company's misdeeds to light."

"That's really good. But are we any closer to figuring out who set the second fire and why the building went up so fast?"

"We are. You know they skimped on the interior walls that could have acted as firebreaks. But they also failed to fireproof the beams before sealing up all the walls. They did some of them, probably what they showed the inspectors, but other than that, they sealed the walls without it, so basically the building was wood-frame construction with nothing at all to stop a fire. It really is a miracle that no one was killed."

"Great, but what recourse do we have?"

"Red and Carter are compiling everything and will give the information to the district attorney. Hopefully he will be able to find a way to bring a criminal case against the company. If nothing else, it should put them out of business."

"And the arsonist goes free," Kevin huffed. "There has to be a way to catch these guys. This isn't the first building they've torched to cover up evidence."

"I know. But we aren't getting very far. No one saw anything other than the flames. There aren't any cameras that caught anything either, so there aren't a lot of places to look. It was a simple fire that anyone could set with a few cans of gasoline and sucky construction already weakened by the first fire. But maybe we'll catch a break."

"Maybe we will. You have to contact Red and Carter. When they make the public statement, I think I need to be there." An idea formed in his mind, one he knew Willy would hate, but it was the only way he could see to bring the people responsible for all this hurt and heartache into the open.

"Why?"

"Willy and I have been trying to figure a way to lay a trap, and I think I just found it." And Lord help him if anything went wrong.

CHAPTER 15

"Are you completely crazy?" Willy asked the following evening as they sat at McDonald's with the kids. Every head in the restaurant turned toward them, including April's and Grant's. April climbed into her daddy's lap to try to calm him, and Grant, who sat next to Kevin, looked like he was going to disappear under the table at any second. "Sorry," he said more softly. "But what are you thinking?"

"We figured we needed a way to draw this guy out, and I have it. The announcement of substandard construction will be made in a day or two. Certain details will be provided that will place the blame on the construction company. We will not accuse them directly by name, but give enough information that they will know we are after them. Red and Carter are going to then explain that the fire department is still investigating, and they'll indicate me without bringing up my name. They'll also allude to the fact that additional evidence is expected soon."

"But that's going to put you in the line of fire," Willy said, his insides churning like a KitchenAid mixer. He pushed back his food and took a deep breath. "They'll come after you."

"Yes, they will," Kevin told him as though it were no big deal. "I want them to. That's the whole idea. I've already made a show of being at my house and walking the dogs, which I'd like to bring over secretly so they'll be safe." He pulled out his phone. "I found this at the house this morning."

It was a picture of another of those awful threats. "And you're acting like it's a good thing."

Kevin nodded. "It means they know where I live and that I'm not staying with you anymore, so you and the kids are safe. Now we just need to bring some heat down on them and we can bring this whole thing to an end. I won't be alone. Chase is going to be with me at the house. We'll sneak him in in the back of my car tonight, and he'll stay with me for a few days. No one will see him. We'll get the dogs out the same way."

Willy swallowed hard. "And if this doesn't work and they…?" He tried not to think about what could happen, but it nearly overwhelmed him. "You could lose everything, including your life." The thought of that was too much, and he turned to look out the window at the cars passing on High Street.

Kevin took his hand, and Willy almost pulled away. "I know this worries you, but I'm going to have a ton of backup. The police will be involved, as will the fire department. Chase will be in the house with me, and I'll have multiple ways to get help quickly. In addition, Red and Carter have installed temporary cameras around the house. They are up and working and face front, back, and through the sides. We've done everything we can to make sure I'll be safe."

Willy wasn't sure he could do this. "I'll take the dogs, of course. The kids have missed them. But…." He didn't want to say something he would regret later. Willy knew Kevin was a firefighter through and through, and he would do what it took to keep others safe, even if that meant putting himself in danger. As much as the idea of Kevin getting hurt scared the hell out of him, he knew he couldn't stand in the way of who he was.

As far as Willy was concerned, Kevin was a hero. He had saved their lives—all of them. And to ask him to turn that off… to stop being who he was… he couldn't do that. So his decision was to either accept that or simply walk away. He clamped his eyes closed because the thought of that made his heart feel like it was being stabbed.

"Okay. I know you need to do this, and it scares me. But you need to be you." He leaned over the table. "Just make damned sure you come out of this in one piece, because if you don't…." He met Kevin's gaze with his best icy stare.

"I fully intend to." He squeezed Willy's hand. "I'll figure out a way to bring the dogs over without anyone seeing. I want anyone who might be watching the house to think they're still there. I actually recorded their barks so they can be played back if someone comes to one of the doors."

Willy sighed. "Then it sounds like you've thought of everything." He sure as hell hoped that was true, because a mistake could cause both him and Kevin a great deal of hurt.

"I've tried to think of every contingency. All we need to do is catch these people. From there we can get them to tell us what we need to know. Right now we don't have much to go on, so it's either trap them or they will be free to do this again and ruin other people's lives."

"I know. I'm just scared for you." And for himself. Kevin was the man he was, but Willy hoped he realized that this little plan didn't affect just him, but the rest of them as well.

"It will be okay," Kevin said, and Willy hoped like hell that turned out to be true.

THE KIDS were in bed, and Willy sat in the living room with a single light on, thinking. Since he'd gotten home from dinner with Kevin, he'd gotten the kids ready for bed. Then, in the quiet, his mind began to race. He knew he had a tendency to spiral out of control at times like this, so he called Evelyn.

"Tell me I'm not going crazy," he said as soon as she answered. He could almost see her rolling her eyes in the silence that followed.

"You aren't going crazy, but you are nuts," she said flatly. "Now what is all this about?"

"Kevin," he said softly. "I can't really talk about the details, but he's doing something that could put him in danger, and I'm worried. It's stupid, I know that."

"That you're worried about him?" she asked. "I don't think so. We always worry about those we love. It's just human nature. The thing is, can you live with the worry in order to have him around? That's what you have to think about. I mean, the choice is simple."

"No, it's not."

Evelyn cleared her throat. "Yes, it is, and I'm starting to feel like I'm talking to my sister when we were six and she'd just taken my cookie." Willy chuckled a little and quieted. It was her turn to talk. "The choice is, do you want Kevin in your life, and all the things that go with it? The amazing man he is, his strength, the way he makes you smile, how good he is with the kids, and how he looks at you? Just thinking about the way, even across the table at dinner with the kids, a single smile in a room full of people could feel as private and heat inducing… as an intimate caress. Put all that against whatever he feels he has to do. Yes, it might be dangerous, but…."

Willy sighed. "He's worth every second of worry."

"Then there. You have your answer." Evelyn sounded satisfied with herself.

"Yeah, I guess I do." So he needed to stop moping and worrying… and he needed to figure out how he was going to help. "Like it was a really tough decision."

"Where is the man of the hour?" Evelyn asked.

"We had dinner with the kids, and then he had some things to do in order to prepare for this setup that he's part of. I don't like it, but I know why he's doing it, and in part it's to keep me and the kids safe. But I… I wish he were here with me now. Not because I want to change him, but just because he makes me feel better just being here, you know?"

"I get it. My nephew melts your butter, and yours needs a really good application of heat." She snickered.

"There's someone at the back door." Willy got up and headed through the house. "It's Kevin," he said when he saw him through the window.

"Then I'll let you go. And don't be scared to turn that heat way up. Call if you need me, but somehow I doubt you'll need me." She ended the call, and Willy unlocked the door and let Kevin and the dogs inside. The pups checked out the bowls on the mat in the corner of the kitchen before spreading out, looking through the house. Willy had little doubt that April and Grant were going to get visitors soon. And Thumper was going to claim his favorite chair.

"Are you all set?"

"Yeah. I made sure no one saw us leave, and I put my car in your garage and came through the yard." He tugged Willy to him. "I appreciate you looking after them and keeping them safe. Nothing has been announced yet, but as soon as it is, I want to have everything in place. I don't know when we can expect them to make a move, but Red and Carter don't think it will take long."

"And the announcement…?"

"Is tomorrow. The chief of police and the fire chief both want to see what we can stir up, so the announcement will be tomorrow afternoon." Kevin held him closer.

"I feel like you're going into battle or something," Willy told him. "I know you need to do this, but I was just on the phone to your aunt, and she explained things pretty well."

"She did?"

"Yeah. I don't need to go into the details, but I need to make a choice…." He looked into Kevin's eyes. "And I choose you over the worry. It's that simple. You make me happy, and I hate it when you're not here and I love it when you are." He wound his arms around Kevin's neck. "And I especially love it when it's just the two of us alone and—"

Kevin growled softly. "I know what you're trying to say, and I love you for it."

Willy stilled. "Did you just say that you loved me?" He had never expected to hear those words again, not after Mark died.

Kevin grinned. "Yes, I did. Nothing gets past you economists." He winked, and Willy kissed away that grin until Kevin moaned softly in his arms.

"I love you too," Willy whispered between kisses. "There's just one issue. We're in the laundry room. I could turn on the washing machine and we could take that for a spin. Or you and I could go somewhere else much more private."

"I'm all for that," Kevin whispered, and quietly they made sure all the doors were locked before silently slipping past the kids' rooms to his own and closing the door behind them. Willy sat on the edge of the bed, with Kevin parting his legs. The held each other, the kisses growing more intense by the second, until Kevin stopped. "Thumper, this is our bed for now." He pulled away and opened the door. Thumper jumped down from the bed and gave them both a doleful look. Kevin closed the door again after the dog padded out, and they were alone.

Kevin approached him slowly, looming over Willy before pressing him back onto the bed with a kiss that touched his soul.

Willy tugged off his shirt and then pulled at Kevin's, which set off a tangle of limbs to get the rest of their clothes off.

"I have thought about you all day." Kevin ran his hands down Willy's belly and along his hip before cupping Willy's balls in his big hand. Willy held Kevin close, groaning through the kiss that sent electric shocks racing through him. "And I want you."

Willy moaned softly. "And I want to feel you in me."

Kevin groaned deeply and nearly dropped the drawer from the bedside table in his haste to get at the supplies. Willy chuckled, and Kevin growled again.

"What? Sex should be fun."

"But not funny."

Willy wound his fingers around Kevin's cock. "There is nothing funny about this." He stroked slowly, and the mirth evaporated, replaced by passion that threatened to blow Willy away. Kevin tugged him to the edge of the bed, parting his legs, and teased his fingers at his opening as he took his cock down his throat in a single swift movement that took his breath away. And when Kevin breached him with a finger at the same damned time, he thought he was going to fly to pieces.

"Kevin," Willy pleaded after the most delicious torture possible. He hadn't thought he would ever feel this alive again.

"What do you want?" he asked, his voice deep and rough, lips swollen and wet.

He pulled Kevin up to him, mashing their lips together as their chests heaved. "I want you to fuck me."

Kevin groaned, and Willy held him tighter, the kisses growing more intense until Kevin backed away and got himself ready. Seconds later, Willy was being kissed again as Kevin pressed to him, and Willy opened himself, taking Kevin inside him. The initial burn was intoxicating, and that sensation only grew as Kevin filled him more and more, his cock stretching him until he felt Kevin's hips against his ass. Willy stilled him, taking the time to adjust and give himself a chance to breathe. Then, slowly, Kevin began to move.

"Which do you like more?" Kevin asked. "Out...?" He drew back, and Willy moaned. "Or in?" He filled him once more with almost agonizing slowness, and Willy's eyes closed. "I just saw my answer."

"Hell yes," Willy whimpered as Kevin continued his slow pace, rolling his hips just right. It was too much and not enough all at once. Kevin was sexy as hell, his chest glistening in the light from the window. Willy loved that sight and could watch Kevin forever, but the rest of him was quickly reaching the point of no return, and as much as he wanted this to last, he could already feel the beginnings of his release sneaking up on him.

Kevin slowed, drawing out the excitement. Willy felt like he was balancing on a knife edge, and Kevin kept him there for longer than he thought possible. He was so close, and just when he thought Kevin was going to take pity on him, he'd slow again, pushing Willy higher and higher, until he could hardly breathe. "I know just how to play your body," Kervin whispered. "You have the sexiest sighs."

"What?" Willy gasped, clutching at the bedding.

"I can tell your need. You want to come so bad, and yet you aren't quite there." Willy knew exactly how he could get there, but Kevin gently batted his hand away. "Your release is mine. I want to give it to you. I want to be the one to send you over the edge so hard that your head aches."

"You're almost there already," Willy admitted, and Kevin pressed forward, stretching his torso and finally stroking Willy hard and fast. "I can tell."

"Yeah. Almost… right there…."

"Hold on for just another second," Kevin demanded, and then he gripped tighter, sending Willy flying, and damn, that was exactly how it felt. Somehow he had grown wings and soared with Kevin right next to him.

Seconds passed, and slowly Willy returned to himself. Kevin kissed him, and they held each other, their bodies still connected, but not destined to stay that way. Separation was quivery, and then they lay together in an amazing sweaty mess, breathing hard and holding each other in the quiet. "I'm glad you didn't wake the kids," Kevin told him.

"Me?" Willy smacked him. "You…." He grinned. "That would have been kind of weird."

"You know, once this is over, you should get a lock for the bedroom, because the last thing we'd want is one of the kids coming in while we're making love." He stroked the hair off Willy's forehead. "I know the kids are the most important thing. They have to be. But the time we're together is ours—yours, mine, and not theirs."

"Amen to that." He scooted closer to Kevin, letting his warmth surround him. "Are you going to stay?"

"Yes. But I'll leave early in the morning and try not to wake you. I want to make a show of being at the house before we make the announcement. I don't know if anyone is watching us now, but judging by the notes we've received, they are paying attention, so we'll do our best to keep them off their game and make sure they're watching where we want them to." He got out of the bed and went to the bathroom, then returned with a towel that they used for cleanup. Then he climbed back into bed and they snuggled together.

"This is where I want to be," Willy said softly.

"Me too," Kevin whispered softly.

"And I want all of us to be safe." It was like he was putting a prayer out into the universe. Willy could only hope that it was listening.

WILLY SAT in his chair and turned on the local news station's noon broadcast. Almost immediately, they announced that they were going live to Carlisle. Willy couldn't help smiling as the police chief stepped to the microphone. Red and Carter stood behind him, along with Kevin, who looked great in his uniform. The police chief explained what they had found and that their investigation was ongoing. However, they had been able to prove that the building contractor had used inferior products and had not followed code. "We're still gathering information, in conjunction with the fire department." He indicated Kevin. "We should have much more information soon." Then he opened the session up for questions, which he answered without giving too much away, instead leading everyone to expect more information in the near future. Even Willy found himself wondering what was to come.

"Is this the big announcement?" Evelyn asked as she entered his office.

"Yeah. They did a good job, and I hope it does what it's supposed to. But I hate the idea of Kevin putting himself out there like this. But it's who he is. The contractor did more work in town, and each of those buildings is being reinspected."

"That's good," Evelyn said.

"Yeah, except you have someone who would burn the building before they'd let anything come to light, so we have to do it quietly and capture the person behind the fires. I hate that Kevin could be putting himself out there to get hurt." But there was nothing he could do. Kevin had explained to him why he was doing it, and he knew it was for the greater good… so that no one else had to go through what he and the kids had. "But he's doing what he thinks he has to, and I love him for that."

"Wow," Evelyn whispered.

"Yeah. He's spending the next couple of days at his home, and I'm staying away. The dogs miss him, and the kids always ask me when Uncle Kevin is going to come to read them stories before bed. They adore him, and so do I. I hate it when he's not at the house with me. Sleeping alone really sucks, and yet I'm worried…."

"You and Kevin have plenty of time to make long-term decisions. You don't need to rush, even if the kids ask you about him every night. You need to take things at your own pace."

Willy nodded. "I'm so damned proud of him for doing this, and scared as hell at the same time. But all I keep telling myself is that he will be okay and that he knows what he's doing. I figure the kids and I will have movie night and maybe even make a tent in the living room with the dogs." And with the distraction, he could try not to worry too much.

CHAPTER 16

KEVIN LAY awake, listening for any sound that shouldn't be there. Carter was in one of the other rooms, and the entire fire department as well as the police were on alert. The thing was, he had already tired of this routine. It has been two days since the announcement, and nothing had happened. He really had thought that some sort of action would be forthcoming. Instead, there had been nothing, and he was beginning to get nervous that he'd misread the situation.

"Have you heard or seen anything?" Carter asked as he passed outside the door.

"No," Kevin told him. "There has been no alert on any of the motion sensors in the yard or along the sides of the house. Maybe they saw through us and didn't take the bait."

"I'm beginning to wonder myself," Carter told him. "I've been going through all the known employees of Kraft and Hobson, trying to see if anyone jumps out at me, and nothing has. I mean, there are some sketchy characters on the payroll, but no one with a history of arson. Most of what I found was petty-type crime and a few guys who are on parole. But if they try anything, they'll be back behind bars."

Kevin got out of bed. "Do you want coffee or something to drink? I was going to try to rest, but it isn't happening."

"Sure. But I think we should look as quiet and dark as possible, so don't turn on any lights, and try to stay away from the windows." It was after midnight, and they were hoping that someone would try something so they could get their hands on them and find out once and for all what the hell all this was about.

"I got it." He went downstairs to the kitchen, started the coffee maker, and grabbed a couple of mugs. He poured the coffee once it was done and returned upstairs to give a mug to Carter. Then he went to his room, leaving the door open and sitting on the side of the bed, trying not to wonder when something would happen.

"With this type of thing, the waiting is always the hardest part. It can sometimes get under your skin. You have to be patient and drink plenty of coffee. Go on to bed and get some rest. If anything happens, I'll get you up right away. There's no sense in both of us sitting up all night if nothing is going to happen." Carter left, and Kevin drank his coffee and then got back in bed.

He thought about calling Willy, but it was awfully late, and he was likely in bed, right where he should be. He did send him a text that he was thinking of him and missing him. Fortunately he didn't get a response, which probably meant he was asleep.

Kevin was about to set his phone aside when dots appeared in the chat window. He waited for the message to come through.

There is someone outside the house. I don't know who they are, but I saw a shadow move across the curtains. Benjamin just raced into my bedroom and is growling like crazy.

Kevin jumped out of bed. "Carter, get someone over to Willy's. There's someone outside his place."

"On it," Carter said as Kevin pulled on his pants. "Don't think about going anywhere," he added.

"But I need to get over there," Kevin told him as he pulled on his shirt.

"It could be a diversion *intended* to get you over there. We stay here. Red is going to check it out with another unit. The fire department is being alerted just in case. So we stay here and see if they try anything." Carter hurried toward him. "One rules of the stakeout is you don't leave your post. Stick with the assignment."

Kevin wanted to protest, but Carter held up his hand as he talked on the phone.

"What's happening?" Kevin said frantically, ready to race to the door as Carter went silent. He shook his head and listened a little more.

"Red is almost there. The other unit arrived, and someone jumped the fence out of the backyard. They are giving chase…." He continued to listen and then smiled. "Kit has the suspect in custody," he reported.

"Good. Is there anyone else?"

Carter shook his head. "They don't believe so, but they're going to search just in case."

Kevin called Willy, who answered immediately. "They got someone, and the dogs are going nuts. At least they aren't barking, but they're pacing through the house, and there are enough flashing lights to wake the entire neighborhood."

"So you and the kids are okay? It's quiet here so far. Carter says I need to stay here and stick to my post."

"Yes, you do. One of the officers needs to speak to me. I'll call you back in a little while." Willy sounded confident. Kevin, on the other hand, was a nervous wreck. He shoved his phone in his pocket and went downstairs, cautiously peeking out without moving the curtains. The front of the house was quiet, with no one moving. Next he checked the side and then the backyard, both of which were quiet.

"Nothing else right now. They have searched around the house and found no one else," Carter explained.

"I'm wondering if this is it or if they were just trying to scare us," Kevin said.

"I wish I knew. Red and the guys will locate a vehicle if there is one and then search it. We'll see how much we can get out of our suspect and then go from there. Maybe this is it, but I'm not particularly hopeful. It feels like an opening move to me, especially since two of the notes came to Willy's place." As much as Kevin hated it, he knew Carter was probably right. Still, he worried that Willy and the kids were in danger, and that sent a chill up his back. The last thing he wanted was to bring this to their doorstep. They had already been through enough.

The scent of gasoline caught in the air, and Kevin stilled. "Someone is here," he told Carter, who got on his phone.

"Code Red," Carter said as they hurried to the back of the house, where the scent was growing stronger. "Accelerant used. Get here now." He turned to Kevin. "Go out the front. Somone will be here in moments."

Kevin glared at Carter. "Bullshit. Come on. We have to get this guy before the house goes up."

Carter pulled out his gun. "Stay behind me," he said softly before easing open the back door. Kevin knew he was waiting for something to happen, but it was quiet… for a moment.

"Fucking hell," someone whispered under their breath out in the yard. "Goddamn roses" followed.

Kevin motioned to exactly where he was. Fortunately the idiot had gotten caught in the wild roses that filled one corner of the yard and were covered in small thorns that grabbed anyone who got close.

Carter made his way to the corner of the house and peered around the edge of the wall. Kevin stayed still, bracing for the whoosh of ignition, his heart pounding, and yet his mind was clear and ready.

"Freeze, this is the police," Carter said. Through the windows in the sun room, Kevin saw the red plastic can drop to the ground, spattering gasoline out of the spout.

The man took off like the hounds of hell were after him, racing for the back gate, which he might have left open after jimmying the lock, but the thing had a tendency to close on its own because of how it was weighted. Seeing his escape route blocked, he veered to the side of the yard and then made a break toward the front. Kevin was ready for him, pushing the fleeing man as soon as he got close enough. He went sprawling through Kevin's barberry bushes and fell against the fence. Carter was right there to cuff him.

"Jesus, this fucking yard hurts," the suspect groused as Carter got him out of the flower bed.

Other officers burst through the gate, with two of them taking custody of the suspect and getting him out of the yard. The fire department arrived next, and they foamed the back of the house. The plants under the back sunroom windows and the siding on that side of the house would need to be replaced, but at least for the moment, everything was reasonably safe.

"How close did he get?" Kevin asked Chase, who stood looking at the foam that was absorbing much of the gasoline.

"All he needed to do was light it. But he really didn't know what he was doing. This was no professional job. If he wanted to set the house on fire, he could have done it closer to the front. Sure, this would have gone up…."

"But it was an addition some years ago."

Chase nodded. "Yeah. We'd have been here before this had a real chance to spread."

"Maybe now we'll be able to learn what was going on and more about why Willy's building and the others were being burned."

"I would hope so," Carter said as he joined them. "The other suspect lawyered up, and we expect this one to do the same. But we can still pit the two of them against each other to see what we can get. Red is pretty good at that sort of thing." He shared a smile with them. "At least we have them, and hopefully we can all sleep a little better at night."

"I sure as hell hope so," Kevin said. He stepped back and pulled out his phone to call Willy. "It's over."

"Did they come there too?" Willy asked.

"Yeah. I think they figured they needed to try for both places to be safe, but we were ready and got them. I'm safe. We did our part to help catch them, and now the police will do their bit to make sure they don't do this again."

"Thank God," Willy said softly. "Are you going to come over?"

Kevin lowered his voice. "Just as soon as they're done with me here." He needed to see Willy and make sure he was all right. He needed to hold him tightly, smell his hair, and feel his smooth skin against his. He had to know Willy was truly okay, and he wasn't going to be able to relax for a moment until he did.

KEVIN WOKE in Willy's bed but found his boyfriend missing. He stretched and listened. Sure enough, laughter and giggles reached his ears. He was safe, and so were Willy, Grant, and April. He missed Willy already, but the aches in certain places reminded him that Willy had been a wild man once they had gotten alone behind closed doors. He had been very sexily insistent on who was doing the driving. Kevin smiled to himself and got out of bed, dressed, and went to join the others.

The kids were at breakfast as though nothing had happened, but Willy was ghostly white and seemed on one hell of an edge. Not that Kevin blamed him after last night. He had tossed and turned next to him for hours. "When is your first class today?"

"Nine," he said softly. "I'll be okay. It was a straining night, but the police got the suspects. I'm sure they haven't learned much from them, judging by the fact that the guy here was already asking for a lawyer before they even had him in the police car."

"Did they find their car?" Kevin asked. He had been too intent on getting to Willy to ask him last night.

Willy nodded. "It was a block away, and they already had it towed and searched it. I don't know what they found, but Red seemed pleased, so I'm willing to bet they have enough to get tall, dark, and creepy to talk."

"Did you see him?" Kevin gathered Willy in his arms just because he needed to hold him.

Willy nodded slowly and looked at the kids. Kevin took the hint and didn't press with more questions. "Red says that he'll call later to provide an update as soon as he can."

"Okay." He wished he knew what he could do to bring this whole thing to an end.

"They did say that once they found the car, they thought that there had been a third person. They said there were signs of someone else but that they couldn't find them. So maybe they got scared off." He sounded hopeful.

"Daddy, who got scared?" Grant asked as he munched on a french toast stick.

"No one. Finish eating so I can take you and your sister to school." Willy's voice was gentle, but there was no missing the nervous undertones. He slipped away and got the kids to finish their breakfast. Then he got them dressed and packed their lunches.

"I don't know what to do," he finally said as he put Grant's lunch in his backpack. "Should I stay home from school in case they come back? If I don't, I'm going to worry that someone is going to come and burn us out of our home again. And…."

"Go on with your life as best you can. I have to go back to my place, but I'll ask Carter about having someone keep an eye on things here." This was turning into a real production. "Don't worry. Just call me between classes, and I'll let you know any updates that I have." He hoped he was giving Willy the right advice. Drawing closer, he pulled Willy into a hug and kissed him. "This will be over soon."

"How do you know?" Willy asked.

"Because both guys in custody are going to want to save their own skin, and that means that they'll flip on anyone they can, so I don't think we have to worry about this any longer. They walked right into a trap, and now we have enough evidence to put them away for a long time. Arson is one thing, but what they did by trying to burn people's homes is likely to be termed attempted murder, and that's going to carry a whole lot of repercussions."

"I know this is over." He released a deep breath. "And I'll be okay. It will just take a little time for the immediacy of the situation to fade." Willy looked into his eyes. "What is it? You look… scared."

"Is all of this too much?" Kevin asked. "I'll understand if it is and if you need to walk away. I get it. This sort of thing is more than most people bargain for. I know that being with a firefighter is going to be…." He didn't know exactly what word to use.

"Special?" Willy supplied, to Kevin's surprise. "How about hot?"

"Who's hot?" Grant asked. "I not hot."

"Just eat your breakfast," Willy told him. "We have to go soon." He finished getting the kids' bags ready and took Kevin's hand. "We need to talk about everything, but not right now. I have to get these two to school, and then I need to get to the college in time for class. You need to go to the fire station and get in touch with the police to find out what's going on. We'll meet back here for dinner?"

"That would be great." Kevin took a quick kiss and then left Willy's and headed to the station. He had plenty of work to do and reports that would need to be made. Nothing was ever finished until the mountains of paperwork were done.

<h1 style="text-align:center">CHAPTER 17</h1>

WILLY ANSWERED questions all day, because apparently the police and the fire department showing up at your house meant that everyone on campus knew about it in a matter of seconds. Evelyn was good enough not to pressure him for details, because Willy didn't really want to talk about it. He would eventually, but he was trying not to think too hard about the fact that he could have lost his home for a second time. At the end of the day, he picked up the kids and got them home for their snack.

"Are you sick, Daddy?" Grant asked as Willy sat at the table with them. "Can I kiss it and make it better?"

"Me too," April piped up, so he got a kiss on each cheek, and he forced himself to smile.

"Uncle Kevin is coming over in a little while."

Grant climbed down and ran to his room. "I get Legos!" He was so excited, and Willy smiled to himself as April finished her snack. He cleaned her up and got her down. She ran off to get her cart and play food.

By the time Kevin arrived with the dogs, the kids were ready, both of them vying for his attention. He hugged each of them and left them to play before coming to Willy with a smile that sent his insides quivering. He grew warmer by the second as Kevin hugged him tightly.

"What a day," Kevin whispered.

Willy held him and didn't want to let go. He wanted to know if the police had anything but was nervous to ask about it, so he stood in Kevin's arms and let the tension of the past few days finally bleed away.

"I can tell you the latest news," Kevin said.

"Sure." He rested his head on Kevin's shoulder, and he slowly ran his hands up and down Willy's back, soothing away the jitters.

"The guys we caught are singing like crazy. It seems Kraft and Hobson has been using dodgy materials for years, but it's been harder and harder for them to cover up, even in Philadelphia, where they seem to have powerful people in their pocket. So apparently when the fire was reported here in town, they sent three people to Carlisle to handle it. The two in custody have given up the third man, and the police are confident they will find him."

"Is that all there is to it? All of this is to cover up things they did over a decade ago?" Willy asked. "I was hoping there was much more to this."

"I don't think so. Sometimes it's all about money, and people will do some pretty shitty things to protect themselves and their cash. But it seems that with what Red and Carter were able to get from the suspects, they were sent by the bosses to make sure that nothing came to light. As near as Red and Carter can figure, all of the buildings they worked on will need to be inspected from top to bottom. They skimped on materials, including the concrete."

"Wow."

"Not only that, but the state police are involved, and they are getting a subpoena for all their records, so it's likely this is going to bring down the entire business."

"Then that's good. No more people are going to have to go through what I did." That was a big deal.

"The thing is, that fire brought all this to light. Not that I would have wanted the fire to happen, but something good did come out of it, and you helped that happen."

Willy nodded slowly. "I know. But I wish none of this had happened. I wish that the kids and I didn't have to lose everything."

Kevin tugged him to him. "I know. Me too. I didn't mean to make light of all you've been through. It's a lot, and Kraft and Hobson is going to pay dearly for that. They are. There isn't going to be anything left of the business once this is all over, and there are going to be a lot of criminal charges. This is going to cost them more than money."

"Good." Willy rested his head on Kevin's shoulder. "I'm glad it's over." He held Kevin tightly. "How much damage is there to your house?"

"Parts of the yard are already turning brown, and the plants against the back of the house are going to die. The department pulled the siding off that wall and had it carted away so it didn't start on fire, and I'm going to need to have all of it reshingled. But other than that, it's going to be okay. These guys had no idea what they were really doing. They figured spreading gasoline around and then lighting it would get what they wanted. But the guy at my house splashed a bunch on himself, so if he had lit the fire, he would have likely been caught in it." Kevin moved back and gently cradled Willy's cheeks in his hands before drawing their lips together. "It's all okay as long as I know you and the kids are safe."

"We are now," Willy said. "I get the idea that we always will be as long as you're around."

"It's all part of the service." His eyes went really dark, and Willy shivered. "As are a lot of other things."

Willy found himself giggling like an idiot as images of Kevin doing wickedly wonderful things to him popped into his head, just as Grant raced over with a bunch of Legos. He shoved his latest creation in the air.

"That's great," Kevin said. "It looks just like a horse."

Grant grinned. "Will you come play with me?"

"Give me a few minutes and I will," Kevin said, and Grant raced into the other room.

Willy shook his head. "He thinks the sun and moon rise with you. Whenever you're gone, he asks when you're going to come back, and the dogs." Willy didn't know quite what to say. "The kids don't understand why the dogs aren't here all the time." He was hoping Kevin understood what he was asking.

"Do you think it's a little soon for us to move in together?" Kevin asked, and Willy nodded.

"I do. But I want you to understand what's at stake. The kids are already beginning to accept you as part of the family. And what they need is stability. You and the dogs being here and then being gone is something they don't understand."

"So you do want me to move in?" Kevin asked.

"Things will happen between us when the time is right. I don't want to rush things, but I do need you to understand that it's more than me and you. If we're going to build something between us, then we need to know what the stakes are."

"I get that. The kids have to come first, and we can't jar their lives. They've already had enough change in their lives."

"Okay, we sound like we're on the same page, but yet I'm not sure. I mean, we aren't ready to live together, and we want the kids to be happy and stable… so what do we do? Every time you come, you bring the dogs, which the kids love. And then when you go home, so do they, and the kids… well, especially April doesn't understand it, because she thinks of Benjamin as her dog." But he was Kevin's dog. Not that Willy thought Kevin should give Benjamin to April; it was just that it was hard to explain ownership issues to a two-year-old who was in love with her puppy.

Kevin chuckled. "It means that we see each other on a regular basis. But we have to understand that things between us are important and aren't going to change. I want to be part of your family, and I want you to be part of mine—you and the kids. So from there we'll figure it out."

"Uncle Kevin," Grant called.

"Go on in to play. I need to get a few things started for dinner. Then, once the kids are asleep, we can talk some more." He hadn't expected this conversation to be this difficult, though he knew why he was having so much trouble. A part of him wanted to just have Kevin move in with them. But it was too soon, and rushing into things wasn't good for him or the kids.

He prepped the salad and veggies. He also prepped the potatoes. Grant had requested mashed, so he got them ready to cook. The tasks gave him a chance to think, and he figured he was being dumb. The kids would deal with Kevin coming and going, just like they dealt with saying goodbye to their friends at school. It was easy because they knew they would see them again soon. And Willy didn't exactly have a revolving door on his love life—he kept watching Kevin with the kids and smiling like an idiot. He was worried about stability while he was dating a real-life superhero.

"Look at that!"

"Yay!" Grant said as Kevin held a super-tall tower so it didn't fall over. Grant handed him bricks until the tower got way too tall and buckled in the middle, sending everything crashing to the floor. Grant giggled, and April put her hand over her mouth as though something was very wrong. But then she laughed.

"You start another tower. Remember how I showed you to do it to make it stronger?"

Grant nodded and got to work as Kevin strode into the kitchen. "Do you know what I want?" Kevin asked. "I want the kids and you in my life. I want to be here for Grant and April's first day of school. I want to see them grow up into wonderful individuals, and I want to be here when you cry on my shoulder as they go away to college for the first time."

Willy glared at Kevin. "I will not cry." Oh hell, who was he kidding? He was going to lose his shit when his kids went away. It was that simple. But he also had a lot of years before that happened. Kevin snickered. "Okay, I might, but you had better not bring it up."

Kevin just smiled. "Okay. I won't say anything in fourteen years when you cry as Grant goes off to college. It will just be something I pretend didn't happen."

"Either that or you'll be too busy trying to look stoic so you don't tear up yourself." Willy couldn't help grinning as Kevin tried out the stoic look but couldn't hold it. "Yeah, that's about what I thought."

"So you see us together at Grant's graduation?" Kevin asked.

Willy put the knife down on the chopping block and lifted his gaze to Kevin. "When I close my eyes, I see us at April's first dance recital. You're the one going nuts with the camera. And I see us together as you teach April to swim. I have the camera that time. Then there's Grant's soccer games and high school plays. Graduation and college follow, until it's just the two of us. Then I see us together, gliding down a river in Europe or sailing off to Australia to get on with our lives while our kids are changing the world."

Kevin came up behind him and slipped his arms around Willy's waist. Willy leaned back slightly, pressing to Kevin's solidity. "Is that what you really see?"

"Yeah. Maybe it's just what I want and I'm jumping way ahead, but yeah. That's what I see. What about you? What do you want?" Willy stayed still.

"When I close my eyes, I see you in bed, eyes shining, watching me. You're as beautiful as you are now, with a few gray streaks in your hair that make you look every bit the distinguished professor. Your eyes are just as bright, but there are tiny wrinkles around the edges that make you look wise. But it's the way your lips part slightly that completes your heated look."

"So you see me old." Willy wasn't so sure how he felt about that.

"I see *us* old—sexy old."

"You're only digging the hole deeper," Willy warned playfully.

Kevin spun him around and kissed the breath out of him.

"I supposed as long as you kiss the me with gray hair and wrinkles like that, I can forgive you."

Kevin held his gaze like a magnet. "I will kiss you like that forever." He didn't say anything more, and they simply started at each other. "So don't worry about a little time now. I'll be here, and once the kids are gone and we're both in our dotage, I'll still be here. So what's a few months to figure a few things out?" He kissed him again, only this time it was more the kind of kiss that lit a fire and then let it settle into the kind of warmth that could last for hours.

"Good." Willy slipped his arms around Kevin's neck, resting his forehead against Kevin's. "Because I want the river cruise *and* for you to still see me as sexy when I'm old. I want all of that, two kids, a house full of dogs, and you. Everyone I love." He swallowed hard as Kevin's gaze grew heated.

"Yeah. Me too. Especially the love part." Kevin held him as the kids seemed to realize where they were and joined them. Grant jumped up and down, and Kevin picked him up as Willy did with April, the dogs milling around their legs, looking for attention as well. It was the beginning of a new life and their new family.

EPILOGUE

"THANK YOU for the cookies, Miss Ellen," Grant told the landlady after Willy had explained their future plans. They had been in the apartment for almost nine months, but their time here was coming to an end.

"Yes, thank you for everything. You came through for us when we needed it most." He was so grateful to her.

"I'm glad we could help. And you were good tenants," she said with a smile. "I have new renters coming in ten days, and I wanted to make sure that you'd be finished moving."

"We'll be getting the last of the things moved today, and I'll be back over tomorrow to clean up. I can give you the keys then so if there is anything you want to do before the next tenants move in, you'll have time."

"That's great," Ellen said, and Willy thanked her again for all her help before she left.

"Go check your room to make sure all of your things are out of it, okay?"

Grant hurried away while Willy gathered the last of the boxes and carried them out to the car. He still had a few things in the one bathroom, and he boxed them up before taking that to the car too. Grant came down with a few things that had been missed, and Willy loaded them up before walking through what had been their home for nearly a year. Once he was done, he got Grant buckled into his seat and they headed north of town to their new home.

Kevin had sold the house he had, and Willy added the money he'd saved. Together they bought a newer home. It had a large fenced-in yard for the dogs, and there was a place for a play structure. The kids each had a room of their own, and the house had a finished basement that they were turning into a family room, complete with a place for all the kids' toys. The house was big enough so that when Willy's parents came for Thanksgiving, there was enough room for everyone.

Willy pulled into the driveway. Grant got out of his seat and ran up the walk to the front door. Kevin came out with April in his arms, the dogs racing out to greet them. "Did you get everything done that you wanted?"

"Yes." He leaned in for a kiss. "The place has all working smoke detectors, and the fire extinguishers are hung. I also finished getting this one's room set up. Grant's is pretty much done as well." He smiled as Grant ran around the yard, the dogs giving chase. He fell on the grass, and the dogs gathered around. Willy hurried over, but the dogs got there first, licking Grant until he giggled at the top of his lungs.

Kevin set April down, and she joined her brother.

"Come on. Let's get the last of this unloaded and inside." They had been working for two weeks to get the rooms painted and the furniture moved in and set up, and now that had nearly been completed. The front of the house had an office, and Kevin had set it up with a desk for him and plenty of shelves for the books that Willy tended to collect. Kevin lifted the biggest box, his muscles bulging. Willy got a smaller one and followed him inside.

"Come on," Willy called. The dogs all raced inside with Grant and April right behind, laughing as they called to one another.

"April's birthday is coming up in a few weeks," Kevin said. "I marked it on the calendar."

"It's during my spring break. I was going to plan a party for her…."

Kevin tugged him into his arms. "I can get that same week off, and I was thinking that we should take a trip with the kids. My mom would love to come on a trip and help babysit."

"I know. But I haven't had the time." He had been working hard these past few months and had finished his economics book and found a publisher for it.

"I know. You've been busy, but we have the time now. So I thought we could drive down to Florida. Mom is already talking Disney." He said the last part really quietly because otherwise Willy wouldn't be able to get the kids to sleep for a week. "What do you think?"

Willy nodded. "I think that would be really nice. But what about the dogs?"

"Chase said that he would watch them for us while we're gone."

"Will we be able to get tickets? It is spring break," Willy cautioned.

"I can. Your spring break is early, so there are still tickets available. We can leave on Friday as soon as you're done with work. I'll sleep during the day so we can drive well into the night." He smiled, and Willy swallowed hard.

"You've really thought a lot about this."

"I have. I want all of us to have a great time and do things as a family." He turned and tugged Willy into a kiss.

"So it sounds like we'll be taking our first family vacation."

"Yeah. The first of many," Kevin said, and Willy nodded and smiled. A family home and family vacations—hopefully without threats or arson. Though truthfully, if occasional drama was the price for having Kevin in his life… bring it on.

Keep reading
for an excerpt from
To Protect
by Andrew Grey

Coming January 2026

CHAPTER 1

"COME ON, Evie," Atlas De Vaus said as he stood by the back door of his small row house on East Pomfret Street. Evie pranced up with her Kong between her teeth. Once she saw he was holding her harness, she set the toy in her box and sat down right next to him. The harness meant that play time was over and that the two of them were going to work. "That's my good girl," he said warmly as he ran his fingers through her thick tan and black Belgian Malinois coat before putting on her harness.

Atlas adored Evie. They had been through K-9 school together, and at first no one thought Evie would make it through the training. It had been tough; early on she hadn't caught on to what they had been teaching. But there was no way Atlas was willing to give up. He worked with her outside of class because she had more heart than any person he had ever met. In fact, Atlas often wished he could meet a guy with as much heart as his dog. He swore the day he did was the day he'd marry. But that wasn't bloody likely.

Evie sat next to him, waiting as Atlas put on his coat, and then they were off. He led her through the yard and opened the door of his Bronco. Evie took her place in the back, and he closed the hatch before getting into the driver's seat, heading to the station.

"Morning," Larry Melvoin said as Atlas and Evie walked in the station together. Evie watched him and didn't react to anyone else. She was working and focused, the way she always was. Atlas had known as soon as he saw her at the training facility that she was perfect for the program. The leaders had already written her off, but Atlas saw something the others didn't, and in the end they had graduated near the top of the class. "Too bad about the other day." Melvoin snickered quietly. The guy really needed to develop some people skills… and fast. "I guess not everyone is perfect."

"Leave them alone," Carter Schunk said as he strode out of the station.

"The only reason you didn't find anything was because you didn't look deep enough," Atlas said. "Evie scented drugs, and you kicked a little bit of dirt and said there was nothing there before moving on." He rolled his eyes. Larry could be a real ass sometimes.

Carter cleared his throat. "Stop it," He snapped and then turned to Atlas. "The captain asked to speak with you as soon as you got in." He tilted his head toward the office, so Atlas headed down the hall with Evie right next to him. He knocked and entered.

The captain was on the phone, but motioned him to sit down.

He ended his call and sat back. "I wanted to be the one to tell you."

"I already got razzed by Larry on the way in." Atlas placed his hand on Evie's back. No one got to call her skills into question. "He was practically gloating."

"Melvoin is jealous because he flunked out of K-9 two years ago. But…." He cleared his throat; it was what he did to change the subject. "Anyway. I sent a squad car back to that scene after I heard what Larry did, and they found a stash of pills and other drugs a foot below the surface in a plastic container wrapped in cellophane. She did good, and I wanted you to know."

"But Larry…?"

"Melvoin is my next appointment," the captain said just as his phone rang again. He answered it and motioned toward the door. Atlas left with Evie along with him, going right to his desk.

Atlas opened his bottom drawer and pulled out a bowl. He added water and set it down for Evie. They were partners, and she relied on him and only him—that was the deal. So in his mind, she came first too. He took her pad from the corner, placed it next to his desk, and Evie curled up like the amazing girl she was. Now that she was all set, he logged in and got to work himself.

It took an hour for him to answer all his emails and submit the last reports from the day before. With all that done, he led Evie out to their K-9 patrol vehicle and headed out. There were limited teams like them, so they had to be ready to go when needed, and their first call of the day came almost immediately. Atlas drove to an address on Louther where he and Evie assisted in a call at the home of a known dealer. They had been trying to nail this guy for months, and as soon as they entered the house, Evie went to a section of living room wall and sat down, looking up at him.

"Right there," Atlas said, pointing.

"Are you sure?" the officer in charge asked. It would mean tearing out the wall, so they had to be right. His belly did a single flip, the way it always did at moments like this, but he trusted Evie with his life.

Atlas nodded and stepped back, drawing Evie along with him as another officer took a sledge to the wall, knocking through a combination of drywall and plaster. A brick of cocaine fell to the floor almost immediately, and the dealer was taken into custody amid a flurry of protests that he didn't know any of that was there. He and Evie checked the rest of the house, finding drugs behind outlets and cabinets in almost every room of the building. Once they were done, Atlas took Evie back to their vehicle, where he fed her and gave her some water.

"You did good, like you always do," he told her before closing up the back of the vehicle and pulling away.

They had gone maybe a block when a call for backup come over the radio from the state police. They had made a stop of a semi on the freeway and needed an additional unit. Atlas waited for a response, but didn't hear one, so he signaled that he was on his way, ETA two minutes. He flipped on his lights and took off, thankfully not needing his siren. He used it as little as possible out of concern for Evie's sensitive ears.

He pulled up behind the trooper's vehicle and got out, recognizing Nelson, a fellow officer. "Hey, Wyatt, what's up?" It was unusual for troopers to ask for general backup like this.

"The truck was all over the road."

Atlas nodded. "Better safe than sorry," he said. "You take care of business, and I'll follow your lead."

"Thanks. Is Evie with you?" Wyatt asked. "You could have her sniff around. I just have a feeling about this one."

"No problem." She probably needed to pee anyway, and this would be a good opportunity. Wyatt went to speak to the driver while Atlas got Evie out of the back. He walked her to the side of the road where she squatted and did her business. Then he brought her up toward the back of the truck, and Evie almost immediately sat down. "Good girl," he told her, waiting for Wyatt to take the driver's license and other information before coming back to join him.

"You need to check the back of the truck."

"Evie found something?" Wyatt asked as Evie panted and managed to look pleased with herself. "All right." He returned to the driver, who came to the back. "Open it," Wyatt said, all business. The driver looked around and grew more and more nervous by the second.

"There's just a load of detergent," he said, his hands fumbling as he opened the lock. Atlas swung the door open to two pallets of boxes side by side, creating a wall. Wyatt called for additional backup, taking charge of the driver. Atlas returned Evie to the back of his patrol vehicle before climbing into the truck. Using his flashlight, he peered over the boxes to a second set of pallets. He climbed over them to what appeared to be empty space. Once he reached the far edge, he angled his light down.

Eyes stared back at him as big as saucers: a group of women huddled together with a slight young man standing in front of them. "You no hurt them," he said firmly, as though he were ready to fight.

"It's okay. I'm here to help. I won't hurt any of you." Holy fucking hell. "I'm going to help you." He slid back, still surprised.

"Was Evie right?" Wyatt asked.

"Oh yeah. Take him into custody," Atlas said flatly. Few things shook him, but seeing those people huddled together, barricaded in there, was enough to make his knees weak. Shit, how in the hell could someone do that to someone else?

"I didn't do anything. I'm just the driver," the man said as Wyatt read him his rights. Then, as other cars arrived, they got the suspect into one of the vehicles to transport him to the station.

"What do we have?" Wyatt asked when he returned. "Drugs?"

Atlas shook his head. "People. The front half the trailer is open, and there are half a dozen people barricaded in there. One man, five women. They seem to be of Eastern European descent, but I'm not sure. We need to get the truck unloaded enough to get them out. I don't know how long they've been in there, but it's been a while, judging by the scent of unwashed bodies."

"Jesus," Wyatt whispered.

"Let me call Social Services. There are local folks who can help them." Atlas pulled out his phone. He knew just the person to call. Chris Joy was amazing and would know exactly how to help these people. "Hey, lady," he said when she answered. "It's Atlas. And I need some of your expertise."

"How so?"

"We have five women and a man barricaded in a truck on the highway. I believe they were being trafficked north, most likely to New York or Philadelphia as domestics, but…." He left the rest unsaid. Chris had seen it all and knew more about the implications than he did. "We are working to get them out, but it would be best if there were women here to help them."

"I got you. Where do you want us?"

"The truck is northbound on 81 just before the York Road exit. But be careful when you get out." He scratched his head slightly as cars whizzed by.

"I'll be there in ten minutes. At least I can try to reassure them that going with you is safe." She hung up, and Atlas knew she would be here in record time. That was how she was.

He joined the others in moving some of the load off to the side, and soon they had a path to the people in back. Atlas climbed into the truck and used his flashlight to make his way back.

"It's okay," he said gently as he reached where the group was. "We aren't going to hurt you."

He shone his light on the floor, but it was enough to illuminate the people huddled together. "Promise?" the man asked. "We are hungry. Need water." Atlas relayed the message, and water bottles were passed to him. He handed them out along with granola bars. They seemed to calm somewhat after that, and Atlas helped them get out. The man watched him warily, helping each of the women to climb out before he followed.

Chris was already there, doing her best to reassure them and helping three of the women to her car and then helping the other two into Atlas's back seat, along with the man, who thankfully was able to translate. Then Atlas followed her as she pulled out.

"How long were you in there?" Atlas asked as he drove. All three of the people kept turning toward Evie as though she was going to eat them. "Evie is the one who found you."

"We were in truck for days. We start in Florida," the man said, his eyes huge. "It very hot and no water." They had all drunk what Atlas had given them, and by the time he pulled in at Chris's building and got them inside in the air conditioning, she had already gotten more water out as well as more food.

"I believe they're speaking Russian, but they could be from anywhere in that region." Chris said softly as she did her best to reassure them that they were safe. He didn't understand a word of what they were saying, but thankfulness was almost universal. The women sat together talking softly.

"What happen to us?" the young man asked, eyeing Evie warily as she sat next to his feet.

"We will find you a place to stay," Chris said. "I'm trying to see if I can find a halfway house that can take them. We have a few who speak some of the Cyrillic languages. I believe they are speaking Russian or maybe Georgian, and I know of at least one place that can help them. But I don't know if they have room." She lowered her voice. "But they will only take the women."

Atlas nodded slowly. He knew a lot of these shelters were for the victims of domestic violence, and a man in those places could be disruptive for women who were trying to put the initial pieces of their lives back together.

"Do what you can," Atlas told her and took a step back so he didn't make everyone else more nervous. The women tended to eye him warily, while the young man stood between them and him like he was the guardian of their virtue. And maybe he was, in a way. They had all been packed in the back of a truck like cargo, and who knew what all of them had been through. Chris hurried away, and Atlas heard her talking on the phone. She made as number of calls and then returned.

"I found a place for the women. The home with a Russian speaker had four openings. But someone is leaving tomorrow, so the fifth room will be available, and I was able to give them dispensation for a night." She seemed a little worn out and wired at the same time. "But I have no place for him."

"They speak Russian and Georgian and I stay with them. Keep them safe," he said, standing as tall and proud as a man a little over five feet could.

"They are going to a safe place for women only," Chris said gently. "They will be fine and no one will hurt them. The woman who runs the shelter speaks Russian. She will try to help them."

He sighed and relaxed slightly. "Okay. I sleep in park or wherever. I be okay. I be okay. You no worry."

Atlas sat down and watched as Chris got the women and, with the man's help, Chris was able to get some basic information about each of the women. Then she got them together and led them out to a van, where another woman drove them away.

"You can't stay in the park or camp out somewhere," Atlas said.

"Then I figure it out." He sounded so confident.

Chris returned and went back to the phones. She made call after call before returning.

"No luck?" Atlas guessed.

"Not right now. I might have space in a few weeks, but at the moment there are no openings unless I put him in Harrisburg, but then he'd be out of my jurisdiction."

"No. I stay here," the man said firmly.

Chris seemed at the end of her resources, so Atlas spoke up. "Why don't you put him with me for a few days? I have the next two days off, and maybe something will open up by then." He couldn't let the guy stay in the park somewhere. There were too many homeless people in town already. "He's been through enough, and I have a guest room."

Chris seemed skeptical. "Are you really equipped for this? I know you're a cop and all, but taking in someone like this is a big responsibility. It's likely he has issues that we know nothing about." Atlas held her gaze, waiting for her to come up with a better plan. "I guess I can place him with you, but I'm going to stop by to check on both of you."

He rolled his eyes. "I appreciate your faith in my abilities."

"Atlas, you're a cop. You give orders and expect people to do what you tell them. You're trained to take charge of a situation, for your own safety and that of others. This isn't like that. He's going to need a gentler hand and a lot more understanding. I just want to make sure you know what you're getting yourself in for."

"I guess I'll find out," Atlas told her.

Chris threw her hands up. "Fine. I'll keep him here for today, and you can pick him up after your shift. I'll stop by tomorrow and the day after to make sure everything is good while I find him a more permanent placement." She hurried away, and Atlas sat down.

"You're going to come stay with me for a few days. Okay? I'm Atlas De Vaus, and this is Evie. She's the one who helped us find you." Evie sat with her tongue out, staying where she was the way she'd been taught.

"I Bazel Dadiani," he said, putting his hand on his chest.

Atlas nodded. "I have to go back to work, but I will come back here once my shift is over, and then we will go home." He stood, and Bazel did the same. Atlas left with Evie and got into his car, hoping like hell that he was doing the right thing. He couldn't just let the man survive on his own. Maybe Chris was right and he was the least prepared person on earth to take someone in like this. But it was too late to go back now.

Scan the QR code below to order.

ANDREW GREY is the author of more than two hundred works of Contemporary Gay Romantic fiction, including an Amazon Editors Best Romance of 2023. After twenty-seven years in corporate America, he has now settled down in Central Pennsylvania with his husband of more than twenty-five years, Dominic, and his laptop. An interesting ménage. Andrew grew up in western Michigan with a father who loved to tell stories and a mother who loved to read them. Since then he has lived throughout the country and traveled throughout the world. He is a recipient of the RWA Centennial Award, has a master's degree from the University of Wisconsin–Milwaukee, and now writes full-time. Andrew's hobbies include collecting antiques, gardening, and leaving his dirty dishes anywhere but in the sink (particularly when writing). He considers himself blessed with an accepting family, fantastic friends, and the world's most supportive and loving partner. Andrew currently lives in beautiful, historic Carlisle, Pennsylvania.

Email: andrewgrey@comcast.net
Website: www.andrewgreybooks.com

THROUGH the FLAMES

ANDREW GREY

Carlisle
Fire

1

A Carlisle Fire Novel

Kyle Wilson hasn't had it easy. His insecurities and nasty home life made him lash out as a kid, and when he finally came out as gay, his family disowned him. Then, just when he's pulled his life together and gotten his construction company running, he's caught in a fire and forced to take costly time off.

When firefighter Hayden Walters rescues a man from a burning building, he's just doing his job. He doesn't expect it to turn his life upside-down, but the man is none other than Hayden's high school bully.

He definitely doesn't expect Kyle to come to the station to thank him in person.

With awkward apologies out of the way, Kyle and Hayden realize they have a lot in common. And when it turns out someone set the fire at Kyle's construction site to target him, they find they can solve each other's problems too: Hayden needs a place to stay while his apartment is renovated, and Kyle doesn't want to be alone in case the firebug strikes again. Things between the two of them quickly heat up—but so does the arsonist's agenda. Can they track down the would-be killer before it's too late?

Scan the QR code below to order.

UP IN FLAMES
ANDREW GREY

Carlisle
Fire

A Carlisle Fire Novel

Newly minted firefighter Chase van Casten has always seen things others miss—except when it comes to love—so when a string of fires pops up at his new job, he knows right away that something isn't right. Unfortunately, the only person who believes him is the owner of one of the burned properties.

Jerrod Whipkey lost everything he owned when his home burned. Investigators determine the fire's cause to be faulty wiring, but as an electrician, Jerrod checked it over thoroughly. Now he's in danger of losing his reputation along with everything else.

While Chase and Jerrod try to untangle the truth behind the fires, the heat between them builds to white-hot. But while Chase keeps Jerrod at arm's length, the arsonist seems to have both of them in their sights. Can they forge a way forward with their hearts intact and uncover the arsonist before they get burned?

Scan the QR code below to order.

FIRE AND FLINT
ANDREW GREY
CARLISLE DEPUTIES
1

Carlisle Deputies: Book One

Jordan Erichsohn suspects something is rotten about his boss, Judge Crawford. Unfortunately he has nowhere to turn and doubts anyone will believe his claims—least of all the handsome deputy, Pierre Ravelle, who has been assigned to protect the judge after he received threatening letters. The judge has a long reach, and if he finds out Jordan's turned on him, he might impede Jordan adopting his son, Jeremiah.

When Jordan can no longer stay silent, he gathers his courage and tells Pierre what he knows. To his surprise and relief, Pierre believes him, and Jordan finds an ally… and maybe more. Pierre vows to do what it takes to protect Jordan and Jeremiah and see justice done. He's willing to fight for the man he's growing to love and the family he's starting to think of as his own. But Crawford is a powerful and dangerous enemy, and he's not above ripping apart everything Jordan and Pierre are trying to build in order to save himself….

Scan the QR code below to order.

FIRE AND SAND

ANDREW GREY

Carlisle Troopers: Book One

Can a single dad with a criminal past find love with the cop who pulled him over?

When single dad Quinton Jackson gets stopped for speeding, he thinks he's lost both his freedom and his infant son, who's in the car he's been chasing down the highway. Amazingly, State Trooper Wyatt Nelson not only believes him, he radios for help and reunites Quinton with baby Callum.

Wyatt should ticket Quinton, but something makes him look past Quinton's record. Watching him with his child proves he made the right decision. Quinton is a loving, devoted father—and he's handsome. Wyatt can't help but take a personal interest.

For Quinton, getting temporary custody is a dream come true… or it would be, if working full-time and caring for an infant left time to sleep. As if that weren't enough, Callum's mother will do anything to get him back, including ruining Quinton's life. Fortunately, Quinton has Wyatt for help, support, and as much romance as a single parent can schedule.

But when Wyatt's duties as a cop conflict with Quinton's quest for permanent custody, their situation becomes precarious. Can they trust each other, and the courts, to deliver justice and a happy ever after?

Scan the QR code below to order.

FOR **MORE** OF THE BEST **GAY** ROMANCE

www.ingramcontent.com/pod-product-compliance
Lightning Source LLC
Chambersburg PA
CBHW071520100726
47908CB00004B/1229